# NELLIE FROM NEWPORT

## OPERATION BIG ROCK BRIDES - BOOK FIVE

## NORA NOLAN

Published by Blushing Books
An Imprint of
ABCD Graphics and Design, Inc.
A Virginia Corporation
977 Seminole Trail #233
Charlottesville, VA 22901

Nora Nolan
Nellie from Newport

eBook ISBN: 978-1-64563-910-7
Print ISBN: 978-1-64563-911-4
v1

# PROLOGUE

*BIG ROCK, WYOMING TERRITORY, MID TO LATE 1880S...*

*D**ear Philip,*
  *We've done business now for nearly fifteen years. I started doing business with you because of recommendations from other ranchers, but I kept doing business with you because you came to be a trusted and good friend and I treasure that. Now I need help, big help. I have a couple of favors and among my circle of acquaintances upon whom I could call, you are uniquely qualified to help me with both of them. It's never been easy for me to ask for help, especially for help of this magnitude, but I'm afraid it's unavoidable now. I'm dying. I'm told I might only have a few weeks.*

  *I need for you to come to Newport to liquidate my livestock and sell my ranch. It might be that other local ranchers would be interested, but I just haven't felt up to the task of talking to them about buying. I'm weak as a kitten and can't even remain standing for more than a few minutes before I have to sit or lie down.*

  *I want you to keep a suitable amount from the proceeds for your* own efforts and put the remainder in an account for my daughter, Nellie. I trust your judgment.

As for Nellie, well, if you thought that last request was a big one, then you'll think this one's a doozy for sure. I would like for you to take her back to Big Rock and find her a husband. You've shared with me how the mail order bride business is flourishing in your town and how many good men there are who would like to find wives.

Several eligible men have moved away from here since that gold lode was found east of the Indian Territory. There are still some men around here, just a few, but I fear her chances of finding a suitable mate are slim. How shall I explain the reason for this? I can only suggest it's because they've met her already. My Nellie has been my prize, my absolute joy, for all these years, especially since her mother passed a few years ago. Now I realize I have done her no favors for letting her get away with doing whatever she wants and giving her whatever her heart desires.

It's taken a bit of persuasion and more time than I care to reveal, but Nellie has agreed to go to Big Rock upon my death and burial, provided you agree to help us in the manner I'm asking. It helped to persuade her somewhat when my own hands said they would not stay on to work if she were running the ranch.

Philip, please understand Nellie isn't a wild beast or even a contrary shrew, at least most of the time. She's quite a pretty girl but sometimes acts as though she's too well aware of it. Some might be of the opinion she's only aware of herself. Underneath it all, I see a sweet spirit inside her. It just needs to be coaxed out and polished up some. She might be in need of a bit of comeuppance. All right, truth be told, there's no 'might' to it. The girl needs the structure and discipline I've denied her all these years.

I do pray you'll find it within you to help me. I'll be completely ready to meet my maker if I know my daughter, the ranch hands and my stock are taken care of.

. . .

*SINCERELY YOURS,*
   *Albert Lancaster*


PHILIP READ the letter as soon as he picked it up from the mail counter at the mercantile. He hadn't been expecting a letter from Al since he usually wired short messages. Philip and his wife, Bethie, discussed it outside in their wagon on the way across the street and down the block to the telegraph office. Bethie reread the letter as Philip went inside to send a wire to his friend.


*WE'LL BE THERE in ten days on the 12th* STOP *We will take care of everything* STOP *Philip Hickam*


PHILIP WAS ALREADY a successful livestock broker a few years prior when he met and married Bethie Benson in Big Rock and decided to live there permanently. His only relative, a cousin named Molly McBride, lived there and he wanted to be close to her. He and Bethie built up their own thriving ranch but he still was an active broker and was often called upon by struggling ranchers for consultation. He'd consulted with Al Lancaster several times over the years as Al expanded his operations.

he Ladies' Aid Society attendees took their seats, some wondering why Bethie's husband had chosen to attend. When Harriet pounded her gavel twice for attention, the group all faced her inquisitively.

She smiled beatifically at them. Harriet always did love an audience. "You may notice we have a visitor this afternoon, and quite a handsome one I might add. Philip Hickam has just today been made aware of a young woman in need of a husband. Philip, I'll turn my podium over to you."

Philip stood and addressed the group. "I received a letter today from a dear friend of mine who has asked me to take care of some things for him. I believe the best way I can explain it is to just read the letter to you."

The group listened attentively and a few twitters arose here and there as Philip read the letter aloud. He looked up when he finished. "So, ladies, you now know as much as I know of this situation. I can tell you that Al Lancaster is a good man whom I consider to be a dear friend as well as business associate. I already wired him and told him that Bethie and I'll be there in twelve days. I hope while I'm gone you can put your thinking caps on and come up with suitable matches for Nellie, at least tentative ones. You all heard what we're up against here."

Harriet stood to be heard. "We'll be looking, Philip, and I'll make it my own personal mission to spearhead the effort. I'll talk to the men. I trust she'll be your guest when she arrives?"

"Ah, yes, she will. She'll stay with us for as long as it takes to find her a spouse."

"I have to ask," Evie Glover said. "What if we don't find one for her?"

"I'll continue to be responsible for her. Bethie and I discussed that. We have that big spread and I might even build her a little house on it if she ends up not marrying. She will have a good deal of money in her own right, and if she becomes disillusioned with our town, it will be difficult to persuade her to stay. I will try, though, because of my promise to her father."

"I'm not worried about her wanting to leave," Molly McBride said, smiling at her cousin Philip. "Everyone who moves to this town loves it. The only people I know of who moved away had to because of a family situation."

"That's true," he said, also grinning, "but you heard the description of her. Who knows what she might do?"

"I suspect," Molly countered, "that Al's going to expect you to step up and free her of some of those bad habits."

Some of the other ladies chuckled at that, including Philip's wife.

Philip took a deep breath and flashed a smirk. "Bethie and I have talked about that, too. We both think I'm equal to the task."

"Well, I hope you can knock some of that behavior out of her before she arrives," Harriet said. "Even so, I think we need to look for a certain kind of prospective groom. He needs to be one who won't be afraid to be firm when it's warranted. I have a few in mind. Philip, give me your opinion. Do we need to make the men fully aware up front of what they might be up against?"

He considered that. "I would want to know, so yes. I can leave this letter with you so they can read it themselves. Reading about her father's pain and concern might soften their opinion of her. Remind them that we don't know how long her father will linger. It might be several weeks, maybe even months, before she arrives. By that time, maybe I'll have had time to, as you said, knock some of that attitude away. Does anyone have any questions? We need to get home, get packed, and get the boys ready to stay with their cousins." He grinned at Molly.

Harriet stood again and walked to the podium. "No, Philip, you two go on. We've got it from here. You two have a safe trip now, you hear? Bring yourselves and that gal back to us, each in one piece, all right?" She smiled and blew a kiss toward Bethie.

"All right, then," Philip said. "Harriet, I'll wire you and keep you updated on Al's condition. That way you might have a better idea of the time frame we're dealing with."

The Hickams left and Harriet picked up another piece of paper. "We have another young woman who would like to come here and make a match. Let me tell you about her. Let's see here. Her name is Lily Holt and she's a schoolteacher. We need one of those, so let's see if we can find a man for her right here in town, closer to the schoolhouse than the outlying areas."

# CHAPTER 2

*NEWPORT, IDAHO NEAR THE SNAKE RIVER, IN THE*
*SOUTHEAST PART OF THE STATE...*

hen they arrived in Newport, Philip rented a wagon and team. Since they didn't know how long they'd be staying, Bethie had packed two large suitcases and one smaller bag. Philip only needed one.

As they rode to the Lancaster ranch, Philip reminded her again of all the deals he'd done with Al in the past and how he always made him feel welcome at his ranch. Bethie asked him how Nellie had acted when he'd visited in the past.

"Most of the time she was pleasant enough. Looking back, there may have been a time or two when she might not have wanted to be there. You know, like Al had forced her to help act as a hostess. At the time it didn't really register. I just chalked it up to her being a teenage girl."

Bethie eyed him with an inquisitive look that held some accusation and mock scorn.

"What?" he said. "Surely, I don't have to tell you that teenage girls can be problematic."

"Well, then it surely is lucky for you that we had boys."

"And I thank my lucky stars for that every day. Anyway, I wasn't around her that much. She was cordial enough when she wasn't making herself scarce. I truly didn't give it much thought then, but in retrospect, I can see hints in her behavior of what Al was talking about."

∽

"PHILIP! Daddy wants to see you right away," Nellie said as she ran across the porch and down the steps toward their buggy. "Please hurry."

Philip helped Bethie down then hurried into the house.

"Hello, Nellie, I'm Bethie, Philip's wife. I'm so sorry we're meeting under these circumstances."

Nellie fumbled nervously with her hands. "It's nice to meet you," she said as she looked toward the house. She was distressed with worry for her father.

As though she suddenly remembered her manners, she turned back to Bethie. "May I help with your bags?"

"No, Nellie, but thank you. Philip can come get them later." She put her arm around Nellie's shoulder and guided them toward the house. "I would like something to drink after that long ride, though. If you'll show me the kitchen, I'll be happy to make us a pot of tea or coffee. Which would you like?"

Nellie looked at her with a nervous smile. "I should be asking you that. I didn't even think of it."

"Oh, honey." Bethie chuckled. "Heaven knows you've got other things on your mind. I'm here to try to lighten your load. Let me do that."

"Mrs. Nelson has been a help. She comes in twice a week to do whatever needs to be done. A little cooking and a little cleaning, and she takes our soiled clothes back to her sister's laundry in town then delivers them back to us. She doesn't like me very much, but since Daddy got sick she's been nicer to me."

Bethie thought she saw Nellie's eyes fill with unshed tears. "How is your father today?" she asked.

Nellie blew out a long breath. "He seems to decline every day. Mornings are better for him. In the late evenings, he seems to forget things and get confused. Last night he thought I was my mother." A couple of tears finally fell.

"It's hard to see someone we love in that situation." Bethie hugged her tighter.

Nellie led her to the kitchen and reached for the kettle but Bethie took it from her. "I'll put the water on. You go on back there with Philip and your dad. I'll find you when I'm done in here."

"All right. Thank you."

Al and Philip were discussing possible purchasers of the property when Nellie walked in.

Al's voice was weak. "Come hold my hand, angel." Nellie pulled her chair up to the bed and sat. Philip was seated directly across the bed from her.

Philip continued the conversation. "If it's acceptable to you, I'll take one of the men with me and ride around to nearby ranchers and see if anyone has interest in buying. I imagine any who are immediately adjacent would be motivated."

"I still don't understand why those men won't work for me," Nellie said as she mildly huffed. "It's ridiculous that I can't simply keep the ranch myself. I'm almost twenty-one years old, plenty old enough to be responsible enough to do it."

Al squeezed her hand. He looked at Philip as if to make sure he was paying attention, then he continued. "We discussed this, angel. Just living here on the ranch and doing as you please doesn't mean you know how to run it. Why, you've never even paid attention when I've gone over business dealings with the men. You wouldn't know the first thing about how to run a ranch."

Nellie frowned. "I can learn. It can't be that hard if..." She suddenly realized it wouldn't be wise to finish that statement.

"Besides," Al said, "you know the men already said they're leaving if you take over. Then where would you be?"

"Those ingrates. After all you've done for them!" She didn't raise her voice but the tone was enough to show her contempt.

"Precisely," Al said. "After all *I* have done." He emphasized the word I. "You, on the other hand, have been nothing but rude to them. You ignore them when they greet you, you turn away while they're still talking to you, and you bark orders when you want them to do something. I let you get away with it and now I know I was wrong to do that. I should have corrected your behavior all those times and taken a belt to you."

"Daddy!" she said, aghast at the thought.

Bethie walked into the room and pulled up a chair. Philip introduced her to Al. After the introductory pleasantries, Al took control of the conversation again.

"Now to get back to what I was saying. I should have taken you in hand long before now. If I had, we wouldn't be in this unfortunate position we're in now. But I'm grateful to Philip for coming to help us. I've already told him, Nell, that he has my full consent and indeed, my blessing, to take you in hand and do whatever needs to be done."

Nellie protested and tried to pull her hand away from her father's grasp. He tightened his grip and managed to hold firm, even in his weakened state.

"Understand, Nellie angel, Philip now has the authority to whip that attitude and those bad manners out of you as he sees fit. I'm telling him right now," he turned his head to look at Philip, "not to let anything slide because you feel sorry for her. That was the mistake I made all these years. No, if you find her manner or behavior distasteful, make sure her backside feels your displeasure. That's what I had to do with her mother. I will ask you to preserve her ultimate modesty. You'll have to get up under those petticoats to make her feel it, though."

Philip tried to respond in a way that would calm the rising tension. "I understand, sir, but perhaps it won't become necessary—"

Al cut him off, "Oh, it most certainly will, my friend. It most certainly will."

Nellie fumed, jerking her hand away from her father's. She stood and stomped. "He has no right to treat me that way!"

"And it has begun," Al sighed. "Philip, you're up. She already agreed to accept your authority several days ago. Perhaps she's forgotten her own promises. Nellie, it's time you learned to keep your own word. A man's word is his bond, and that expression means the same for women. If you don't keep your word, no one will ever have any respect for you. If you won't keep your word, we'll have to keep it for you. Starting right here, right now. Philip, take off your belt. Nellie, bend over the foot of my bed and pull up your skirts."

"I'll do no such thing," she said as she headed resolutely for the door.

But Philip was faster and he latched on to her arm. He wasn't rough; he'd only grabbed her hard enough to stop her from exiting. "Maybe it's time, Nellie. Come back in here and mind your father. He's given me a task and I intend to see it through. It doesn't much matter if I have your permission or not." His voice held no anger, no accusation.

Bethie tried to be helpful. "I have experience here, Nellie. Don't make it worse than it needs to be."

Nellie jerked around to look at Bethie. "You mean, he's... you've..."

"Oh, yes, many times, especially in the beginning. My advice is to get it over with and move on."

Nellie's heart pounded at finding herself in this embarrassing situation. She hadn't been spanked since her mother was alive, and here she was, a grown up woman, about to be belted while her bare legs and barely covered backside were exposed to everyone in the room. Her tears fell as she tried to accept her predicament. She knew she wouldn't get out of it; she'd never seen her father like this. Philip gently guided her to the foot of the bed. She fumbled at bringing up her skirt and petticoats up to expose her bloomers, so Bethie helped. Nellie bent over the bed, hands resting beside her father's feet. Her eyes were closed, yet tears still fell.

"I expect you to mind me and to mind Philip when he tells you to do something. I expect you to treat him and his wife with respect. I expect you to treat everyone with respect, including the hired hands. I expect you to keep your word. Most of all, if Philip decides intervention is needed, you won't fight him or try to run. Do you understand that?"

Her eyes remained closed. *Just do what you have to do to get it over with.* "Yes, Daddy."

"All right then, Philip, get on with it."

LATER, in the kitchen, the conversation was stilted. Al was napping and the rest of them were going to have a cup of tea.

Nellie couldn't look Philip or Bethie in the eye.

"I wasn't expecting that to happen, especially on our first day here," Philip finally said.

Nellie took a deep breath and started to speak but didn't. After a moment, she did it again. She didn't know what to say and hoped they would realize she was trying to temper her words so she wouldn't appear contrary or resentful, even though she did still resent the situation.

"You don't have to say anything, Nellie," Bethie assured her. "We know this is new to you, and it's happening while your father declines. That's an awful lot of emotion to have to sort through all at once. It might not seem like we're here to help, but we are."

"Does he do that to you a lot? I can barely sit down."

Bethie laughed. "That was one of his lighter ones. I could be quite the rebellious and rudely opinionated thing when I was younger. But I grew up with a father who belted me so I already knew what to expect."

"Opinionated? He whipped you for having your own opinions?" She looked across the table at Philip with disbelief, even horror.

"I'll answer that," Philip said. "No, I enjoy hearing her opinions. She's the smartest person I know and she has insights I don't have. I can spend hours in conversation with her, and indeed, we have many times. But I'm not going to listen to her yell them at me accusingly or spit them out in anger to our friends, or even in front of them."

"Well, I guess that makes sense," Nellie allowed.

Bethie laughed. "I finally realized I had power over that belt by acting the way a grown woman and wife should. It was an enlightening truth to learn."

Philip winked at her.

"Mmm," was all Nellie said, but she said it thoughtfully.

"You've been through a lot today and your father's resting comfortably. Why don't you go lie down? I'll let you know when supper's ready," Bethie said.

Nellie downed the rest of her tea and excused herself.

Bethie stood and walked behind Philip's chair. She rubbed his shoulders. "Are you all right, hon? I know that wasn't how you wanted to start a relationship with her."

"No, but I didn't have a choice. Al must have thought it was necessary. Maybe he wanted to impress on her that he's expecting more of her behavior now that we're here. He's probably right. It had to be done to show her some limits from the start."

She bent to kiss his cheek. "Why don't you go meet the hands while I fix supper?"

Philip pulled her down onto his lap. "I sure am glad you came with me. I wouldn't want to be doing this by myself."

"I'm glad I came, too. The poor girl. She's about to lose her father and the only home she's ever known, only to be carted off to a strange place to find a husband. I don't envy her those circumstances. She'll need a good friend by her side."

"The guest room they always give me is at the end of that hall on the right. Fair warning, I plan for us to make good use of that bed tonight. You'll have to concentrate on being quiet."

"You know I can't do that."

He grinned. "Oh, yes. I know."

PHILIP AND BETHIE understood completely when Nellie wanted to eat her supper in her father's bedroom and help feed him at the same time. She wanted time alone with him now that those precious times were numbered.

When she brought their supper dishes back into the kitchen, Bethie suggested she go on and rest, but Nellie didn't want to do that. "I don't know what it is, but I feel like I need to keep moving. I need to do something with my hands. How about you wash and I'll dry and put away?"

"That will work just fine. Did Al eat very much?"

"No, he's eating less and less every day, even with each meal. I don't think it'll be very long now. It's hard to say it, but I hope he doesn't linger. I can't stand to see him suffer."

Bethie searched for the right words to say. "Maybe he'll join your mother soon," she said softly.

Nellie nodded as the tears welled in her eyes again. They silently washed and dried most of the dishes until Bethie heard a small sob escape from Nellie. She dipped her hands in the rinse water and picked up a towel to dry them.

"Let's leave the rest of these, Nellie. I can do them later or Philip can finish them. Let's you and I go sit on the porch for a while."

"All right."

Bethie poured two more cups of coffee and carried them outside. She waited until Nellie sat before handing her one.

"Nellie," she said softly, "tell me what's hurting you the most."

Nellie's whimpers turned to full sobs for a few moments. When she was able to talk, she did so haltingly. "It's just that all these years, I've been such a disappointment to Daddy. I never realized he thought I was so spoiled, or that I behaved so badly that even the ranch hands didn't like me. I never knew, and now it's too late."

"Oh, no, no, Nellie, that's not the case at all. You are, and you've always been, your father's greatest joy. He told us so himself. You've never been a disappointment to him."

"He did? He told you that?"

"Yes, he did. In the letter he sent to us, I believe he called you his prize, his absolute joy. You weren't a disappointment all these years, you were his bright star, his sunshine, especially after your mother passed away."

A smile shone through Nellie's tears. "He said that? Really?"

"Yes, he did."

"Thank you for telling me that. It's comforting to know."

"He loves you as much as a man can possibly love a child." She paused and tentatively grinned. "I suspect he thinks he loves you too much, so much that he's coddled you instead of setting limits for you."

Nellie nodded as she wiped away tears with the dish drying cloth she still held in her hand. "Yes," she said as she managed a grin of her own. "I do believe he thinks he spared the rod and spoiled the child." Her grin went away. "I've never been as embarrassed and humiliated as when he had Philip punish me today. At the time I thought he was being cruel, both of them. I've thought about it, and now I think he wanted to set expectations going forward. You know, to let me know what the roles will be from now on and that he expects Philip to do what he couldn't. Daddy wasn't being cruel. It was the only way he knew to get through to me in a short time."

"That's insightful," Bethie said. "Philip and I had a similar conversation earlier. He didn't want to do it, but Al apparently thought it necessary. So Philip did as his friend asked."

Nellie glanced sideways at Bethie. "If you're going to tell me Philip's heart wasn't in it, that dog won't hunt. It hurt."

Bethie laughed out loud at that statement. "Then I should warn you not to rile Philip. Believe me, it can hurt a lot worse."

When they went back into the house, they found Philip had finished tidying the kitchen. They both thanked him and Nellie took Bethie's coffee cup.

"I'll just wash and put these away and then I'll be off to bed." She paused. "I'm glad you're both here."

"We are, too, Nellie. Good night," Philip said as he took Bethie's hand and headed down the hall.

THE NEXT DAY, Philip took the ranch foreman, Ray, with him to visit the nearest ranches. There were two owners who expressed serious interest in purchasing the ranch and even agreed to keeping on the existing hands. One even suggested that Ray and his family could live in the ranch house. Philip promised to get back to both of them with specifics on the property and live-stock so they could agree on a price.

When they returned to the ranch, Philip asked Ray and the hands to inventory the barn and other outbuildings.

When he reported back to Al, the older man was immensely

pleased. He seemed to rouse for nearly an hour, then the excitement of the good news must have worn off because he lapsed back into labored breath and weakness.

That evening Nellie helped her father with his supper, but he only ate a few bites before drifting off to sleep. She took their dishes and joined Philip and Bethie at the kitchen table.

Nellie sighed as she sat down. "He thought I was Mother again."

Philip nodded slowly. "I want to go ahead and iron down the purchase agreements while Al's still lucid enough to sign papers. The owners will still give us plenty of time to take care of what we need to."

"You mean bury Daddy and clear out of the house?" There was a bit of sarcasm and resentment in her voice.

Philip eyed her levelly. "Yes, but I wouldn't have worded it so harshly. The buyers didn't. They were both understanding and even gracious."

Nellie let out a long sigh. "I didn't mean to sound bitter," she said.

"Nellie," Philip said and paused to get her full attention. "We all process grief differently. I think it's normal to feel everything from bitterness to sadness to disbelief to anger. It's a highly emotional time. What you just said is all right to say to Bethie and me. But please think before you say something like that to anyone outside this house. They might not understand. Can you do that for me?"

Nellie nodded at him and her respect for him grew a little. "Yes. I can. I will."

"Thank you," he said with genuine appreciation in his voice.

It was a few moments before Nellie spoke, and it was with some apprehension. "Philip, I need to face the reality that I'll be moving soon. How much, I mean, how many of my things can I take? I could be preparing some while Daddy's resting."

"That's a good question, and I'm glad you asked. I want you to take everything that's important to you. Your clothes and personal belongings, of course, but also take things that are special to you. If it's too much to put in our house, I'll store it safely. I imagine some things that belonged to your mother have special meaning for you. Some things that belong to Al do, too, I'm sure. We can ship whatever you want to keep. Don't worry about anything being too much."

Nellie's wet eyes showed her gratitude. "I'm going to need some shipping crates."

"I saw some lumber in one of the sheds. I'll get the men to build some. It won't take long at all."

"Daddy has a lot of nice clothes and boots. Do you think the men might like to go through them and see if they can use any? I mean, after he's gone, that is. I don't want to insult the men, though, in case they think it's charity. We can donate the rest to the church."

"That's a nice idea. I can handle it so they won't be insulted," Philip said. "I've heard of people being superstitious about wearing a dead man's boots. We'll see what happens."

DAYS PASSED SLOWLY as she watched her father decline, but when Nellie remembered they were her last days with her father, her perspective changed. They seemed to pass far too quickly.

She spent a day or two identifying the items she wanted to keep. There were kitchen items, some furniture, her mother's writing desk and her sewing machine, and other such items. She wanted to take every book in the house; her parents read to her when she was young and instilled in her the wonder of escaping into books or reading about famous people. She wanted to keep all of her mother's handbags and reticules and her embroidered handkerchiefs. There were lovely embroidered tablecloth and napkin sets she wanted. She worried that Philip would think it too much, but he said it was all fine, even when she initially culled something and later decided she wanted to take it.

Special crates had to be built for some of the items, such as the velvet loveseat. Smaller crates were built for the books since they were so heavy. When a good load was ready, Philip wired his cousin-in-law and best friend, Derek McBride, to let him know when it would arrive in Big Rock. As it turned out, the loveseat crate was so big, Derek ended up having to send a couple of ranch hands to Rawlins to fetch it. Everything else made it on the stagecoaches.

Each time she watched a wagonload of her cherished belongings ride away, Nellie felt as though a piece of her childhood was leaving. When she realized they would be awaiting her in Big Rock, a peace came over her. In a way they would be there to welcome her home, to her new home.

But in those unguarded moments when she let her long-held attitudes surface, she resented the hell out of having to leave this place she called home.

# CHAPTER 3

*BIG ROCK...*

*H*arriet Smithers sat down at Evie Glover's kitchen table. Evie was the deputy's wife. The sheriff's wife, Amy Larkin, was already seated and was cutting the pie she'd brought to their morning tea visit. They tried to get together like this as often as they could.

"Well, I've spoken to several of the men in town who seem to be the most motivated to marry soon," Harriet said. "They're willing to meet Nellie but most don't seem optimistic that they'll find a suitable match in her. Not too many men want to be married to a spoiled brat."

"I was a little afraid of that," Amy said.

"Whom all did you talk to?" Evie asked.

"I talked to Zeke Warden and Jeb Pardee at the mine. Ken and Jesse Becker over at the sawmill. Oh, and Bart Green at the mill, too. Flynn Connelly at the assay office. Axel Archer at the saddlery."

Evie grinned. "Those Becker twins are such handsome men. I

always thought it would be funny if we could match them up to twin brides."

Harriet chuckled. "That's not very likely, and besides, they'd need to be well-behaved twins. Those boys weren't keen on a woman who acts childishly."

Amy jumped in. "You don't have a good feeling about any of the men being a match for Nellie? Surely, there's a man in town who's not afraid to step up to the task."

"Well, there's one I'm optimistic about. Wes Hollicker."

"Oh! I like him a lot," Evie said. "I remember when he first came to town looking for the cousin he didn't know he had until his mother passed away. I liked him immediately. Yes, I think he'd be a fine match. And handsome to boot! I don't think he'd be one to shy away from a Nellie-type problem. You know, his cousin Ruby stayed with us until she found a husband." Evie chuckled again. "Ruby started out with a behavior problem, too."

They all grinned at the memory. Ruby had been a ruffian sentenced by a judge in Rawlins to come to Big Rock and find a husband within a month. She'd found Jake Jernigan within a week.

"Yes, Wes is our best hope now. He didn't seem to have a problem with the thought of having to keep her in line a bit if he has to. And I did remind him that Philip and Bethie would probably have a calming effect on her even before she arrives. I'm sure he knew what I meant by that," Harriet added.

Evie got up to bring the second pot of tea to the table. As usual, Harriet added a dash of whiskey to her cup.

"So do you think we should interview more men or put our faith in Wes?" Evie asked.

"We can talk to more men, definitely," Harriet said.

Amy grinned. "Or maybe we could talk to Wes more. Create even more desire in him to meet her."

Harriet and Evie both looked at Amy and grinned. They both appreciated a good idea when they heard one.

～

THE NEXT DAY Derek sat on one of the benches in front of the stagecoach office waiting for some more of Nellie's things to arrive. His wagon was parked nearby, out of the way of the stage.

He was engrossed in his newspaper when he heard a horse arrive and its rider say, "Whoa." He looked up in time to see Wes Hollicker dismount. Derek stood to shake the man's hand in greeting, then they both sat on the same bench.

"I'm waiting on a letter," Wes said. "What brings you here today?"

"I'm picking up more of Nellie Lancaster's things that Philip shipped."

"More? There's been a lot?"

"Oh, I guess it hasn't been that much, overall. A few heavy things, though. I don't know what's in this shipment." Derek chuckled. "Actually, I don't know what's been in any of the shipments. I haven't opened the crates."

"Well, I can pitch in some muscle to get it in your wagon. I guess the hands help out once you get it all to Philip's?"

"Yes. They do. Thank goodness."

"Derek, do you have any word on the old man's condition? Any idea how much longer it'll be before Nellie's here in town?"

"I know Philip found a buyer and he paid a good price for the ranch. Lancaster is declining fast. Philip was glad to get the sale nailed down and he got a lawyer out there to finalize the paperwork and do the man's will before he lost his faculties. I get the idea the girl's settled down some. Why, are you interested in marrying her?"

"Maybe. I'd at least like to call on her some and see if we get along."

"You weren't put off by the letter her father sent? Didn't it say the men in town wouldn't marry her because they'd met her?

That's a pretty powerful statement right there, whether she's settled down or not."

Wes grinned. "Yes, it is. Powerful indeed. But, no, I think I can handle a contrary woman if I have to. Besides, I like some spirit in a woman. I'd rather have one with fire in her than one whose flame's been put out."

Derek grinned, too. "I agree, some spirit is a good thing. Just be careful you don't let it get to the point of defiance or bull-headedness."

"Yes, sir, you're right about that. Sure wish we knew when to expect them."

Derek looked at Wes and gave him a knowing grin. "He'll let me know so I'll be here to meet them. As soon as I find out, I'll ride out to your place and let you know."

"I hate for you to do that since I'm about forty minutes in the wrong direction for you."

Derek shrugged. "The horse does all the work."

*Newport, Idaho, several days later...*

It was quiet on the ride back from the cemetery until Bethie spoke up. "I thought that was a really nice funeral, Nellie. There surely were a lot of people there. Your father was highly thought of around here."

"It was nice, wasn't it? That was Daddy's favorite scripture, too, so that made it extra sweet. He's happy in Heaven with Mother, now, don't you think?"

"I like to think so," Bethie said. "The Good Book says there's no sadness in Heaven, so I believe they're happier than we can even possibly imagine."

Nellie was silent then and Philip and Bethie took their cue from her. It was a companionable and sympathetic silence, not an uncomfortable one.

When they arrived back at the ranch house, Philip asked Bethie to cut a piece of one of the cakes a neighbor had brought. He'd take care of the horses and put the buggy in the barn then he'd come in.

"Will do, hon. Do you want coffee or tea with it?"

"Tea. And a big glass of milk, too."

On the way into the house, Nellie asked Bethie if she thought it was really necessary to wear black all the time after a family member dies.

"I never really thought so. People mourn in their hearts and minds and souls, not in their clothes. It's just an outward show. Back home, back east that is, spouses are expected to wear black for a year. I only have one completely black outfit and this is it. I'd have to spend a fortune on black clothes if we lived like that."

"Good. I didn't want you to think I wasn't being respectful to Daddy if I change out of these clothes."

"Oh, goodness no, Nellie. As soon as I get that kettle on the fire, I'll go change, too. I think on a day like this, comfort is more important. Wear whatever makes you feel better."

THE THREE OF them sat at the table, the center of which held a buttery lemon pound cake. Mrs. Stanton, the wife of the man who'd bought the ranch, had brought it over the day before, along with a chess pie and two fresh-baked loaves of bread.

"I'm glad you two are here with me. I don't know if I could have handled all the arrangements on my own. I've never had to do anything like this before. I was still a child when Mother passed, so nothing was expected of me."

"I'm glad we're here, too, Nellie. Al wouldn't have wanted you to be alone," Philip said.

"You could have handled it," Bethie said softly. "I imagine most people feel that way about certain things until the time comes when they have to do it. We do what we have to do. Nellie, you're stronger than you think you are."

"I hope you're right about that," Nellie said. It had taken a few days of being with them, but Nellie finally realized the Hickams were indeed there to help. Her father had truly been trying to lighten her load.

"If Daddy hadn't written to you, I can't imagine what shape the ranch would be in. The men wouldn't have stayed. Where would I have been then?"

"Good thing your father knew that," Philip said.

Nellie allowed a small smile. "Good thing he knew you. You know, I can never repay you for all you've done for me and for Daddy. I know he told you to pay yourself something out of the ranch proceeds, but you didn't take anything."

"There's nothing to repay, Nellie. Besides, we don't need the money. Al was a friend of mine. A good friend. You do things for friends," Philip said with a modest shrug. "You just do."

She looked at Philip and a small, wry smirk curved her lips. "The first day you got here, I would never have imagined saying this, but you're a good man, Philip."

He chuckled and looked down at the last few bites of cake. "Thank you. And I understand completely."

Nellie sighed and the mood changed. "When do you think we need to leave here?"

"There's no hurry. Stanton reminded me again at the funeral that there's no rush. He knows Ray and the hands are taking care of everything. He told Ray that since he has no family to use it, he and his family can move into this house. Are you all right with that?"

Nellie nodded. "Yes. Daddy thinks... well, thought the world of Ray. He's been with him almost since the beginning. It's fitting. But I still have the question when do you think we should leave?"

"I'm leaving that up to you, Nell. Do you think it'll be hard for you to leave this place?"

"It's the only home I've ever had. So many reminders of Mother and Daddy. That's good and bad, though, isn't it? In my mind I know I need to make a clean start. I have to do it. My heart isn't too sure."

Bethie put her hand on Nellie's arm. "You'll know when the time's right."

"The reading of the will is tomorrow," Philip said. "We'll do it here at ten in the morning. The lawyer's notified everyone who needs to show up. I know Ray and the men were asked to be here. And Mrs. Nelson. That'll be the last bit of business we have to take care of for your father's estate."

THE READING of the will went without a hitch. Nellie imagined her father's voice as the lawyer read the words. The ranch ownership was already finalized so the will consisted mainly of bequeaths from his sizable bank accounts.

Ray and the ranch hands were stunned and elated when they learned the amount of money left to each of them. It was enough for any of them to leave the ranch and buy a modest house of their own if they wished, but none did.

Mrs. Nelson also appeared shocked at the amount Mr. Lancaster left to her. She could have saved her meager wages for years and not amassed that much money. She wept unabashedly.

Everyone snickered and it blossomed into belly laughs when the attorney read a certain section, a part that even Nellie laughed at because in her mind, she could see and hear her father saying it. "To Philip Hickam, I leave the sum of two thousand dollars because I know damn well he won't take any money out of the ranch proceeds like I told him to."

The mood in the room turned somber and sad when the attorney read the final passage.

"To my precious daughter, Nellie, my angel, I leave the remainder of the money in both my bank accounts. It's more money than most young ladies will ever see, and I hope you'll trust Philip to be your advisor in financial matters. I've always put my trust in his knowledge and guidance and we've flourished. I wish I didn't have to leave you, my precious angel, but the Lord above knows what is best. Remember, He sees the big picture. In time perhaps you'll know why He called your mother and me Home when he did. I can go peacefully because I know we'll be reunited on the other side. I love you, my dearest Nellie."

Even the attorney's voice caught as he spoke and his eyes welled with unshed tears. After a pause for everyone to collect themselves, he handed out bank drafts to Mrs. Nelson, Philip and the ranch hands, who still hadn't fully absorbed that they were well off, far more so than any other hands they knew.

Mrs. Nelson, Ray and the rest of the hands left soon after, excitedly talking to each other once they were out of the house.

"I didn't ask Ivan Jenkins at the bank for a draft for Nellie," the attorney said. "It's a very large sum and I felt sure you'd rather wire it to your local bank than carry a draft. He's expecting you to come in at your convenience and he'll arrange it."

"Thank you," Philip responded. "What about your fee?"

"Oh, Mr. Lancaster already took care of it and other miscellaneous things, too. There's nothing left to be paid to anyone."

"Well, I thank you again. I appreciate your willingness to have the reading here. I'm not sure when we'll be leaving, but we might not see you again."

The lawyer extended his hand. "Happy to do it. Good day, Mr. Hickam."

~

BY SUPPERTIME THAT NIGHT, Nellie had reached a decision. "Philip, I'm ready now to start over. I think the will reading was what I needed to get me to move on. There's nothing left for me here. I can be ready to go whenever you say. All I need to do is pack my remaining clothes and the few items we haven't sent yet."

"All right, Nellie, I think that's wise. Tomorrow, we'll go into town and stop at the bank to get your money wired to Big Rock. I'll cash my draft, too. Don't let me forget to wire Derek. We can leave the next day."

"Good. I would like to go to the cemetery one last time and say goodbye to Daddy. It's silly, I know, but I do."

"It's not silly at all, sweetie," Bethie said. "I would want to do it, too."

"I'll tell Ray and he can send someone to tell Stanton so he'll know when we're leaving. While we're out tomorrow, we can stop and let you say goodbye to your closest friends in person."

Nellie paused and looked up. "I don't have any friends."

Not one to want to let a mood sadden, Bethie said with a hearty laugh, "Well, you do now, like it or not."

~

*BIG ROCK...*

Derek left the newspaper/telegraph office and headed straight for Wes Hollicker's ranch. Wes was in the pasture and when he saw Derek ride up, he walked over to the gate to meet him.

"Hello, Derek. I take it you got a wire letting you know when they'll arrive?"

Derek's broad grin answered in the affirmative for him. "I did, just now. They'll leave there day after tomorrow and be here in twelve days, on the sixteenth."

Wes grinned, too, and nodded.

"I take it you'll be at the stage office to meet them?" Derek asked.

"Something like that. I'll definitely do something like that."

"You've got it bad, my friend. I hope it works out for you and Nellie."

"I'm confident it will. I plan to make it work out."

"Make it work out? How do you plan to do that?"

"I think I'll give myself a head start. I need to go to Rawlins and meet with someone there. I can time it so I'll ride the stage back with them."

"My friend, that's brilliant," Derek said. "You'd better make a damn good impression."

Wes laughed. "I almost always do."

∾

*Newport, Idaho...*

The ranch hands came out to say goodbye to Philip, Bethie and Nellie. Ray sat in the back of the wagon with the luggage. The bench seat only sat three adults and he didn't mind sitting back there. It was almost as comfortable as the seat, which was to say that neither felt very comfortable for a rider.

When they had covered only about thirty yards, Nellie stopped Philip. "Wait! I have to do one more thing." She jumped down even before the wagon came to a complete stop.

She called out to the ranch hands. "Men, please, come back." She walked quickly toward them and stopped when they met. "I want to apologize for my behavior all these years. I didn't think of anyone besides myself and I'm ashamed now at how I treated you. Well, you and just about everybody else. It was inexcusable, but I hope you can forgive me anyway. I wish I could start it all over again, but I can't. Nor can I stay and prove to you I'm no longer that rude and wicked girl. Please understand I'm so, so sorry and I wish you all the best in life. I truly do."

The men looked surprised but only one spoke up. "Miss Nellie, it was nice for you to apologize, it couldn't have been easy for you. So nice, it would be rude of us not to accept. We wish you all the best, too." He stuck out his hand to shake hers.

She shook it, but she impulsively stood on tiptoe and kissed his cheek. She went through the entire group of them, calling each by name and kissing his cheek. She felt sure some were surprised that she even knew their names. When she'd kissed them all, she went back and climbed up on the wagon seat, a smile on her own face.

"It felt good to do that. Come clean, that is. I just couldn't leave them with such distasteful memories of me."

"That was a nice thing to do," Bethie said. "I'm sure they appreciated it."

"Oh, shoot!" Nellie said. "I meant to get some pocket money while we were at the bank. Will we have time to stop?"

"We do, but your accounts are closed. You don't have any money there anymore."

"Shoot! I forgot."

"No need to worry. I cashed that draft for two thousand dollars and that's more than a whole train load of people will need."

"But that's your money. I have money of my own now, you know. I don't want to be dependent on you for everything."

"That's admirable but not necessary right now. I'll pay for anything you want. Whatever you want."

"But I wanted my own. I want to carry my own money, in my own bag."

"What are you going to buy? There aren't any shops on the train, and I'll handle all the gratuities. We'll only stop for meals, fuel, and water, and they're usually short stops."

"Well," Bethie said, "some of those meal stop places had things to buy in them. Snacks and little handmade things. One or two had a store next door. It's possible we might find something."

"See? I'll need my own money," Nellie said.

"You ladies aren't getting out of my sight when we get off the train. I'll be right there. I'll buy you whatever you want. Everything, I'll pay for everything you want."

"I want my own," Nellie said in a playful, pitiful voice.

Philip's playful voice matched hers. "You aren't about to start defying me already, are you? And us just barely starting out on this journey. I'm wearing the same belt, you know."

Ray chuckled in the back of the wagon. Al's bedroom window had been open that day Philip arrived and the men who weren't out riding the fence line heard everything.

"Absolutely not, I would never do that," Nellie continued. "I was just appealing to your better nature to have mercy on me, an unfortunate young woman who has to leave the only home she's ever known and head to a strange, distant place and wed a man—"

"Good grief, stop!" Philip said, cutting her off and laughing. He handed the reins to Bethie while he reached into his inside jacket pocket and pulled out his billfold. Here, here's fifty dollars. That's more than you can possibly spend between here and Big Rock." He placed the money in her hand.

Bethie looked at him with expectant eyes and held out her hand.

"You, too?"

"I can't let that poor thing shop alone."

Philip handed her fifty dollars. "Ray, do you need pocket money, too?" he hollered to the back of the wagon but Ray declined with a big guffaw. Philip put his billfold back in his jacket and took the reins again.

"I'll pay you back when we get to Big Rock," Nellie said. "I want to spend my own money."

"Yes, ma'am," Philip conceded.

When they reached the railway station, Ray and Philip unloaded the bags and Philip tipped the porters who carted them off to the baggage car. Philip and Ray shook hands and Ray handed the bag of snacks his wife had prepared for them.

"Be sure to thank your wife for this. And I hope you'll keep me posted about how the ranch is doing under Stanton."

"I'll do that, Philip. Look, I want to thank you for all you did for Al Lancaster. He was a good man. You take good care of his little girl, now. I hope you'll let us know how things go over in Big Rock, too."

"I will, Ray, I surely will."

Before Ray climbed up to the wagon's driver's seat, Nellie came running up to him. "Ray, I want to tell you how sorry I am about the way I've acted all my life."

"There's no need to, Miss Nellie. I was around your dad so much, I kinda saw you through his eyes. You were everything to him."

"I know that now. I don't know why I didn't see it then. It's hard to believe how self-centered I was. I plan to keep in touch with you and your wife. Tell her I said goodbye and I'll miss you both."

"I'll do that," Ray said. Before she let him step up into the wagon, Nellie pulled him down so she could kiss his cheek.

NELLIE WAS in the same Pullman sleeping car that the Hickams were in, in the unit next to theirs. Once they all got settled in and the train began to move, she went to their car to visit.

"Have you traveled much by train, Nellie?" Bethie asked.

"I never have. I've been trying not to act like a wide-eyed youngster, but it's pretty impressive."

"I'll never forget my first train ride. My parents and I were traveling from Baltimore and that's when I met Philip's cousin Molly. She was moving here to marry a man she'd only met through letters. She's probably my best friend now. Philip's the one who introduced them, again, by letter. Derek had been a long-time client of Philip's and they were good friends. When Derek's first wife passed away, Philip wanted to introduce his widowed cousin to Derek. And as they say, the rest is history."

"Oh, that's a good story. Since we're sort of on the subject, I know what we can discuss on this trip. Philip, I want you to tell me everything you know about every eligible man in town."

He laughed. "There are a lot of them, but it certainly won't take twelve days to tell you everything I know about them. I could probably do it in twelve minutes."

"All right, then you'll have to tell me about all the interesting people in Big Rock. Surely, there are some."

Bethie laughed. "Now that might take twelve days."

"The train has a refreshment car, but they don't serve meals. They almost always have water and coffee made and if you get there before they run out, they might have cold snacks. Things like cookies or bread and cheese. I propose we go now and explore. Shall we?" Philip asked.

When they got to the car, Nellie was amazed to see a table along one side with recessed areas for pitchers so they wouldn't topple if the train were to surge forward or stop suddenly. There was a long thin loaf of bread and two different types of cheese. A short stack of very thinly sliced roast beef was in another recessed area. They each cut a small slice of bread and the ladies only wanted cheese with theirs. Philip took one of the beef slices, too. They each poured a cup of coffee and sat at an empty table by a window.

As the ladies took tiny bites of their snack and Philip gulped his in two bites, Nellie asked him about the town.

"It's smaller than Newport. I guess that's expected since it's not on a bustling river. We'll get off the train at Rawlins, that's a fairly big city, and take the stage the rest of the way. It's two more days by stage. We'll spend the night at a little stop called

Cooper's Gap on the way. The sleeping accommodations are dormitory style, ladies in one room and men in another."

Bethie interjected, "And he grouses to me about that every time we stop there."

Nellie laughed. "What about the businesses in town?"

"Well, the first one you'll see is Mama Mary's Restaurant, just across the street from the stage station. Mary is one fine cook, I'll tell you that. We'll go there directly from the stage office because it'll be lunchtime and it'll take over an hour to get to our house. I'm much more pleasant company on a full stomach."

"I'll have to remember that," Nellie said.

"Nell, that's true of every man I ever met," Bethie said.

Philip continued, undaunted. "There's a general store, a hotel, a newspaper office that's also a telegraph office, the sheriff's office, of course, a blacksmith, a dressmaker, a barber who's also the undertaker, a silver mine and an assay office, a sawmill, a furniture factory… What am I leaving out, Beth?"

"Let's see, we have a wonderful doctor, a nice saloon and one that's not so nice, a livery stable, oh, we have a community center now, a Methodist church, a schoolhouse, and Wyatt Anderson just started a nice big hog farm."

"I can't believe I forgot the hog farm. I got the hogs for him," Philip said, shaking his head at his own forgetfulness.

"What's the deal with the two saloons? I'm not sure I ever heard of a nice saloon."

"The Buckin' Bronc is the nice one. There are no women of ill repute there," Bethie answered. "The Big Rock Poker Palace is the other one. It does have, shall we say, soiled doves working there. Philip even takes me to the Bronc sometimes, it's that civil. Every once in a while, they have traveling music acts there. The owner is a lovely woman named Tallulah. Sometime when we have lots of time, I'll tell you the story of her and her sister, Hattie, and how Hattie came to be in Big Rock. Philip even played a part in it. But it's a long story."

"Well, it's a long train ride. We'll have to make time for that. I'd love to hear it," Nellie said.

"You can tell her about all the mail order brides. They're interesting stories," Philip said.

"I guess I'm technically not a mail order bride since I haven't been corresponding with any prospective grooms," Nellie said, sighing.

"No, your father sent the mail. But, technically," he said, using her word, "you qualify because Harriet Smithers is involved and even as we speak is probably rounding up men to introduce to you. She's the president of the Ladies' Aid Society and heads up the mail order bride efforts."

Nellie's face went pale. "Oh, no, no. I can't imagine what she must be telling them. I'm afraid if she tells the truth, it might frighten men away. Nobody at home wanted me."

"That may be true of the men who've known you all these years," Bethie said, "but we've known you for these last few weeks and we see you turning into a lovely young lady."

Philip laughed. "Most of the time, anyway."

"I think when they meet you, they'll be delighted," Bethie continued. "And they should be. Just think, you have an education and you're smart, you can cook, you can clean, you're a good conversationalist, you have a sense of humor, and on top of all that, you're very pretty."

"Mrs. Nelson always said I knew I was pretty. She said I acted haughty."

"Is it true?" Bethie asked.

Nellie looked away and then looked back at Bethie. "I'm ashamed to say it probably is. I just never realized how I appeared to other people. She said I tried to boss people around too much. And that I argue too much."

"Oooh," Philip said. "Those last two aren't good. Not too many men want to be around bossy and argumentative women.

If you can't control those two things, they're going to get you in trouble."

"What makes you boss people around? What makes you argumentative? What things to you argue about?" Bethie asked.

"Well, I find myself arguing about women's suffrage. Susan B. Anthony toured Idaho and was speaking not far from us. I wanted to go hear her, and I wanted Daddy to go hear her, too. But he said he was too busy to leave the ranch. I don't believe that for a minute." Her voice began to rise. "He didn't think women needed to bother with voting, that politics is men's business. Now how ridiculous is that? Women live in the same world men live in, and laws and ordinances affect them, too. We should have a say!"

Philip leaned forward. "Nellie, do you realize how much your voice rose when you spoke? Maybe that's part of the problem. Bethie used to do that. Remember when I talked about the way she voiced her opinions when we first met? Rudely? I didn't like that. And I put a stop to it."

"Yes, he did," Bethie said. "Besides, women have been voting in Wyoming since 1869, so you don't have to worry about that issue."

"You vote?" she asked Bethie.

"I certainly do."

Nellie looked around thoughtfully. "Hmm. I'll be able to vote. I like that."

"Let's not get sidetracked. We were talking about situations where you're bossy and things that make you argue or get loud and belligerent. What else do you argue about?" Philip asked.

"Well, I hate to see people do the wrong thing or do things wrong. If I don't tell them, how will they know they're wrong?"

"Are you so sure they're wrong?"

She looked at him blankly.

"It just might be that what you think is 'wrong' is simply different from your way or your opinion."

"I suppose so," Nellie said slowly.

They finished their tea and took their cups to the self-bussing sink area where they'd seen others put their used cups. On the way back to their Pullman car, a porter let them know that the supper stop would be at 5:30. The ladies decided they'd rest until suppertime.

~

THEY DISEMBARKED for supper at a settlement that had little more than a place to provide meals for the train riders. There were a handful of houses and one small building that looked like it might be a store for absolute necessities. They speculated that was where mail was dropped and delivered, too. Nellie was disappointed that there was no place to shop, but even she admitted the food was good.

"All right, Philip, you never did tell me anything about any of the single men in Big Rock. Tell me about a few of them now," Nellie asked as she put a forkful of a cheesy chicken dish in her mouth.

He grinned. "Yes, ma'am, I'll do my best. Let's see. There are several who work at the copper mine, a few more at the sawmill. One or two at the furniture place, oh, the hog farmer I told you about, and two or three ranchers. You know, the ranchers might be the best for you since you grew up on a ranch."

"I don't know. I might be ready for a change."

"Fair enough. First, though, let's talk about money. All the men make a good living. Some of them, though, might be old-fashioned enough that they won't appreciate marrying a woman of means. Your money might make them feel inadequate."

"Oh. I was thinking I'd need to be on the alert for the kind of man who'd only marry me for the money. You know, like a lazy type or an opportunist."

"Yes, there's that, too. I'm going to be checking them all out in that regard. I won't allow you to marry either of those types."

Nellie cocked her head. "Allow me?" she repeated questioningly. "I don't get to make up my own mind?"

"Al asked me to help you find a husband. I intend to do just that, Nellie."

"There probably won't be a problem," Bethie said, softening the mood. "Nellie, I imagine your own instincts will steer you away from insincere men or any with bad intentions. Besides, I don't think the men I know would be like that at all."

"Maybe not. But let me be clear. I'm not going to marry a man I don't want to marry."

"We're all agreed on that, Nellie," Philip said. "I wouldn't expect you to."

There was a stilted silence for a few minutes as they ate. Philip finally spoke again as though there hadn't been any unpleasant words. "Come to think of it, Wyatt's single, too. He's the hog farmer. But he's a little older, nearly fifty. I assume you'd prefer a man closer to your own age?"

"I think so. Maybe up to ten or twelve years older. But fifty's too old for me."

"All right. Let's see, the men at the sawmill. There are the Becker twins, but I don't think either one of them have a temperament to match yours."

"I agree," Bethie said. "I'm not sure it's temperament. They don't seem to have much of a sense of humor that I've noticed. Other than that, I suppose they're pleasant enough." She added in a lower conspiratorial voice, "Pity, too, because they're quite attractive."

Nellie smiled at that.

"I think they live at the boarding house." Philip laughed. "We forgot the boarding house when we listed the businesses in town. You know, that will affect your marriage plans—whether or not the man already has a home. You could live in the boarding house for a short time, but I can't imagine a newlywed couple wanting to do that for very long."

"No, I wouldn't want to live there. All right, we'll cross out the Becker twins for now. Who else is there?"

"Well," Philip said, "Bart Green works for the sawmill, too. One of the strongest timbermen there. Good man. He attends church and he's a friendly sort. Oh, Amos Cameron is another one there. I like him a lot. He and Will Wharton are both single, and best friends. They bought big lots right next to each other on the outskirts of town, helped each other build their houses. I think both of them are excellent prospects. They both go to church, too, most of the time. I think that's it for the sawmill. Well, there are more, but probably not well suited for you. A couple of older ones, too."

"All right, three lumberjack possibilities from the mill. That's promising. Who else is there?"

They heard the whistle that meant it was time to reboard the train. Once on board, they stood outside the entrances to their units and said their goodnights. Before Nellie entered her quarters, she reminded Philip he'd have to finish telling her about the single men the next day.

THE FIRST MEAL stop the next day was at a larger town, and the stop would include water and fuel. That meant it would be a longer stop. The women were delighted that the town had a dress and milliner shop next door to the restaurant. They ate hurriedly and ran to the store.

Both of them ran right past the proprietress and when they realized it, turned back to her.

"I'm so sorry," Bethie said, "we're in such a hurry."

The woman laughed. "You must be riding the train. Don't worry, we get train customers all the time. I'll be at the register ready for check out in case you find something. I won't let you miss it."

"Neither will I," Philip said from the door.

"I usually offer husbands a chair, but I doubt you'll be here that long," the owner said good-naturedly.

"I hope not, ma'am, but thank you, I'm fine. These two have gone a few days without shopping and the distress has taken its toll, I suppose." He waved his hand around the store. "This is medicine to them."

"It's our duty to help each other. I hope I can provide immediate and long-lasting relief for them," she said, making them both laugh.

Without time to try on dresses, the ladies quickly held them up to each other and determined which ones would fit and which ones looked the most flattering. Between them, they bought five dresses, two bonnets, a hat and three shifts. The owner was true to her word and Philip had them herded back onto the train in plenty of time for departure.

That afternoon they decided to go back to the refreshment car, and Nellie hinted it was a good time to finish the discussion about the single men in Big Rock.

"All right, let's see, I think I covered the men at the mill I think would be most eligible. There are a few at the mine, too. Zeke Warden is a good man. He came from Colorado, I believe, and had a big family there. He's fun to be around; he can spin a yarn like nobody's business. He'll keep you laughing."

"Oh, I think I'd like that," Nellie said. Her father had been a gifted storyteller, too, and she'd always asked him to retell her favorites. "We'll call him a strong possibility. Who else?"

"Jeb Pardee, he and Zeke are good buddies. I don't know him as well since he's not quite as outgoing as Zeke, but he's good-natured and I haven't seen or heard anything that would scare me off from him. Those would be the best ones for you, I think. Now there's Flynn Connelly over at the assay office. I think he's around thirty. Another good man, educated, too. Graduated from college and probably knows everything there is to know about ores and metals and the mining business. He could be a good match for you."

"What exactly are you basing your opinion on of who would be a good match for me?"

He smirked. "I'm thinking of men strong enough to handle you and who also have patience and humor."

Nellie rolled her eyes. "I guess that's fair."

Philip leaned over to get her attention. "Now about that eye-rolling... it's fine to do in a light-hearted conversation like this where everyone knows it doesn't mean anything. Bethie used to roll her eyes when she wanted to argue with me. Suffice it to say she doesn't do that anymore. Do you understand? Most men don't much like that."

"Oh, all right. I understand. I'll be careful."

"Good." He leaned back. "Now there's Axel Archer over at the saddlery and leatherworks place."

"Yes!" Bethie exclaimed. "He's an artist with leathers."

"He really is," Philip said. "Beautiful saddles. He also makes small things, too, like coin purses and billfolds. He made mine. It was a Christmas present from Bethie." He pulled out his wallet to show her.

"I agree, it's nice workmanship. All right, who else?"

"I saved the best for last. Wes Hollicker. He's a rancher. I know you said you might want a break from ranching, but living with your father on a ranch and being a rancher's wife are two different things. Wes is a good man and I know him better than the rest of the men. I helped him get his herd and develop a plan for expansion later."

Nellie smirked again. "So I take it he's strong, patient, and good-natured?"

Philip smiled back at her. "He is. He's built up a fine place since he came to town."

"How long ago was that?"

"Not long, about a year, a little more. Year and a half, maybe. He hired a lot of help in the beginning to get a head start on both the ranch house and the barns. He could afford it. That's another reason he'd be a good match for you. He already has at least as much money as you have, probably more. He inherited quite a bit and then when he sold his family home in Dodge's Summit, he split another small fortune with his cousin. His cousin who, by the way, is another one of our mail order brides and lives on the ranch right next door to Wes' place."

"That sounds like an interesting story," Nellie said.

"It is," Bethie interjected. "You wouldn't believe her story. I'll tell you that one, too, when we have plenty of time."

# CHAPTER 4

*RAWLINS, WYOMING TERRITORY...*

$\mathcal{W}$es Hollicker had already checked out the bulls he was considering buying, and he'd met with an older couple that had befriended his cousin Ruby. He gave them a gift Ruby made for them and had sent for him to deliver. His business in Rawlins was complete a day early. If he'd rushed, he could have made the stage back to Big Rock, but that wasn't his plan. He wanted to catch it when Nellie would be on it, and their train wasn't coming until the next day.

Wes knew there were several other men eager to find brides. His hope was that they'd be leery because of what her father's letter said about her, that she was undisciplined and spoiled. He hoped they wouldn't want to take on a wife they'd then need to "raise." That didn't frighten Wes at all. He knew he could handle it and was fully prepared to do just that.

Maybe he even looked forward to it. He wanted a partner in life, a loving and faithful one, yes, but he wanted one with spirit and spunk. A reasonable amount of it, that is. Where would the fun in life be if his partner in this journey were no more exciting than a docile mouse? No, he wanted occasional fireworks. He craved occasional fireworks, needed them.

In the letter, Nellie's father said she was pretty. That was a bonus to Wes. He'd always thought the inner person was more important than external appearances, but truth be told, he was glad she was pretty. Her father said she needed structure and Wes reasoned that a rancher's wife would just about have to live a structured life, considering the housework and outside chores that had to be done. He didn't mind Nellie having some help to do the work, particularly backbreaking laundry, but he certainly expected her to keep his house livable and mostly clean. *Their house.* He didn't know if she cooked and did housework before since her father was a wealthy rancher, but it didn't matter. He could teach her. She only had to be willing to learn.

How willing would she be, not only to learn new things, but to marry in the first place? It was her father's directive for her to marry, but would she do as he wished? She'll presumably be a woman of means now after inheriting. Would she feel the need to marry soon?

What if we don't hit it off? *Well, old self, that's why you're giving yourself this advantage of being in an uncomfortable enclosed space for two days. You'll both know by the time you reach Big Rock whether or not to pursue a relationship. Who knows? Maybe it'll be love at first sight.*

～

*ONBOARD THE TRAIN...*

"Can you think of anything else I need to know about the town? Or the people?"

"I think you'll find them all to be welcoming," Bethie said. "I did when I first came."

"I did, too," Philip said. "They're a good bunch of people. There are one or two characters in the mix," he said with a grin.

"Oh, tell me, this sounds good," Nellie said.

"Let's see, the minister and his wife, the Copperfields, are quite nice, as you'd expect. They're good friends of ours. There's Mary at the restaurant, great cook. Little short round lady who loves to hug and feed people. The Kellys are good friends of ours, too. As a matter of fact, Nessa Kelly was Bethie's best friend growing up. She was our first mail order bride. Angus Kelly is a man you can't miss. He's about six-feet-eight-inches tall, a giant of a man. A strong one, too. In a fight with an ox, I believe he'd win, he's that strong." Philip laughed. "And he has the brightest red hair you've ever seen."

"So does Nessa; they're quite a pair," Bethie said.

Philip continued. "The sheriff, Jim Larkin, and the doctor, Elliott Larkin, are brothers. The deputy, Aaron Glover, and his wife Evie are our good friends, too." He laughed. "As a matter of fact, we were there when they got married. It was sort of on the spur of the moment."

Bethie laughed, too. "That's another story you need to hear. We'll get Evie to tell it to you. She'll have you howling."

"This town keeps sounding better and better."

Philip laughed. "And we haven't even told you about Arthur and Harriet Smithers. They're probably the most, um, how would you describe them, darlin'?"

"Hmm." She thought a moment. "Most memorable. She's president of the Ladies' Aid Society and spearheads the mail order bride operation, so you'll definitely meet her. You'll like her immediately; everyone does."

"What's so memorable about her?" Nellie asked.

"I think it's better for you to discover that yourself. She and her husband will most likely give you a special gift. They give all the couples the same thing."

"Oh, what is it?"

"A surprise," Philip said with a grin.

~

THE LAST EVENING aboard the train was pleasant, but Nellie was anxious; she wanted that choo-choo to chug faster. Ever since she'd heard some details about a few eligible men and the descriptions of the townspeople, she wanted to get to Big Rock quickly. It would be a far cry from her existence back in Idaho where no one wanted her company.

*I can do this. Now that I'm aware of how I acted, I can be on guard and make sure I don't act like that again. I'll pay attention to people. I won't try to boss people around. I won't walk away from them just because I'm bored. I won't treat people like I'm better than they are even if, even if, well, even if I am. Sometimes it's just an inescapable truth, right?*

*The men sound interesting. I'm not sure I'd like a miner coming home to me every day, though. Dirty work, dirty men. There would be so much cleaning, hard cleaning. I'm sure it's honest work, but still. Underground in the mud and the muck all day. No, I don't think that would make for a pleasant existence.*

*But a lumberjack? Timberman? Carpenter? That could work for a decent union if they're as nice as Philip says they are. Strong possibilities.*

*The assayer? I don't know a thing about ores or mining, but if he's educated and smart, he might be good.*

*The one with the leather place, the saddlery. I like that. Fresh leather smells so good. But what if he does any tanning there? I hear that stinks to high Heaven. No opinion until I know if he'll ever come home and stink up the place with his clothes.*

*The rancher? Maybe. It would be nice to do something different, be in different surroundings other than a lonely ranch all day, but he did sound promising. At least I could be assured he doesn't want me for my money.*

Her thoughts were interrupted by a knock on the door. She heard Bethie's chipper voice call out, "Nellie! Open up."

She did. "Philip and I are restless. Want to go to the refreshment car again and see if they have coffee or tea available?"

"I would love to," Nellie said as she walked out her door and closed it behind her.

There was no coffee or tea left this late, but they were pleased to find pitchers of water. They were particularly pleased to find chipped ice in the insulated recess that kept it mostly frozen.

"I'd like to have had a bit of tea, but this ice water is refreshing. This has been a treat for me on this trip, to have so much ice available," Bethie said.

"Yes, it's wonderful in your drink, but not quite so nice when it's underfoot," Philip said.

"Daddy bought us baseball shoes to wear when it was icy. You know, the shoes players wear with metal spikes on the bottom," Nellie said. "Makes all the difference in the world. You don't need them when there's snow, but if it's solid, slick ice, there's nothing better if you have to get outside." She grinned at them. "I didn't really *have* to get outside, but Daddy bought me some anyway. Sometimes you have to stomp down to penetrate the ice if it's a hard freeze, but it works."

"That's brilliant," Philip said. "You know, there's a cobbler in Rawlins. I think I'll check and see if he can come up with a way to have spiked boots for icy weather."

"You aren't wearing those in the house!" Bethie's look was one of stern warning.

"Good point. Maybe he can make removable spikes," Philip added as an afterthought.

They were silent a moment as all three drank their water. Philip got up and brought the pitcher over for refills before putting it back and sitting again.

"As much as I hate riding on that bumpy stage, I'll be glad to see the end of this train ride," Bethie said.

"Me, too," Nellie responded. "I'm glad I bought two new dresses. I'm going to wear one tomorrow to celebrate the end of the train ride, and I'll wear my favorite one the next day to celebrate arriving in my new hometown."

"I think I'll wait to wear my new one the day we arrive home. There will be so much laundry when we get home," Bethie lamented.

"Do you do your own laundry? We had most of ours sent out to our housekeeper's sister who has a laundry business. There was always something that needed to be washed anyway, so I know how. I can help with laundry," Nellie said, happy to be offering to do something useful.

"It's about the same at our house. We send most of the clothing out and some of the bedding, but with the boys, there's always something that needs to be washed."

"I bet you'll be glad to see your boys. I'm eager to meet them."

"I have missed them, but believe me, they'd rather stay and play with their cousins than come home." Bethie laughed. "Though I'm sure Derek and Molly will be thrilled at our return. Their life can get back to normal. Our boys can be boisterous."

"I haven't been around many children. I was an only child and there were no other children close by. The single ranch hands lived in the bunkhouse, but the married ones lived in their own homes. I know very few children." She paused. "I think I've only seen children at restaurants or when we went to church occasionally."

"Living with us might be trial by fire, then," Philip said with a laugh. "Nellie, I got to thinking earlier today, I'm afraid I've given you short shrift in my thoughts about finding a suitable husband for you. I never once asked what kind of qualities you would like to have in a mate, and I should have. I'm sorry for not asking your opinion. Tell me now, what would you like your husband to be like?"

"Oh, well," Nellie said. She brightened at his honesty then

wrinkled her brow in thought. "You mean physically, or are you talking about character traits?"

He shrugged. "Both."

"Well, physically, I would like for him to be taller than I am. And strong. That may sound shallow, but I do. He doesn't have to be handsome, but I'd prefer that he at least be pleasant to look at. As for what characteristics I'd like, I want what I imagine most women want. Someone who's patient, enjoyable to spend time with. I like to laugh, so I'd like someone else who does, too."

"I'm glad you mentioned patient," Philip said. "I agree. No one likes an impatient person in any case, but let's face it, it's really important for you."

"Philip," Nellie started to whine but, instead, said it reasonably and was proud of herself for doing so. "Other than that first day when Daddy insisted, you haven't had to get after me for anything."

"That's true, and I'm grateful, but a lifetime of habits are hard to break overnight. There will be times when old behaviors pop up. You need to recognize that when your husband takes you to task over something, it doesn't mean he isn't patient. It means you've probably exhausted his supply."

She forced out a heavy breath, too heavy to pass as a sigh. "Fair enough. I suppose you're right. But I was thinking about that very thing right before you two knocked on my door tonight. I'm going to do my best to act with much more grace than I ever have before. I never realized what I was doing to myself and how it affected others who were around me."

Bethie patted Nellie's arm. "Good for you, Nellie. I'm proud of you."

Nellie giggled. "I remembered what you said about realizing you had the power over Philip's belt by acting the way you should."

Bethie let out a laugh, a loud one. "Well, if you learn nothing else from either of us, learn that!"

# CHAPTER 5

*RAWLINS...*

ellie waited with Philip and Bethie in their Pullman unit as the train slowed to a stop in Rawlins. Nellie had spent extra time on her appearance that morning and as a result, her long hair was neatly arranged on top of her head to complement the new hat she'd bought a few days earlier. Bethie hadn't taken quite as much care, but she looked lovely in a new bonnet that matched her dress.

"Ladies, I'll make sure our bags get on our transport to the stagecoach office. We'll eat lunch at a restaurant near it; I've eaten there several times. The food's good and they'll make us snacks for the stage ride."

They disembarked and Nellie commented on how her legs felt a little funny being on solid ground after being on a moving train for so many days.

"I think that happens to a lot of people, especially if you don't travel much," Philip said. "It may take a few hours for your legs to adjust. I recommend standing or walking as much as you can before we depart on the stage."

They were taken to the stagecoach office where Philip checked them in and made sure their bags made it on the coach. He checked the clock on the wall against the time on his pocket watch and was gratified to see they both said the same time.

"We have plenty of time to eat and I want to take care of some other things, too. Would you ladies like to walk with me up to that building across the street on the far corner? It's the telegraph office. I want to send a message to Derek."

"Yes, I'd like to walk a bit. I'll be sitting for the next two days," Bethie said, not exactly complaining.

"If you don't mind, I think I'll stay here. I promise to stay right around here. If you look over, you'll see me."

Philip grinned. "I don't see why not. Just don't run off with any men before I have a chance to check them out. We won't be long."

"I'll be here." Nellie watched them go and the thought struck her that they truly were her good friends now. That made her smile.

"Now that's a fine thing to see after a long ride with no company but a horse. A beautiful woman with a heartbreaking smile." The man flashed his own grin and tipped his hat to Nellie.

She looked around nervously and wished Philip was there. Was it proper to respond to a stranger who was flirting with her? Especially one this handsome? This *manly*?

"Oh, um," was all she could get out. Her eyes grew wide.

The man took off his hat. "Please, ma'am, I'm sorry. I didn't mean to be forward or make you uncomfortable. I was only trying to pay you a compliment. You must hear them all the time. Mine probably sounded clumsy."

"Oh, no, no," she said, not wanting him to feel bad. But she couldn't figure out what to say that would sound right. Finally, she spoke. "To tell the truth, I don't hear it. There weren't many people in my small circle where I'm from. It was a very small circle. Just my father, actually."

The handsome man flashed another grin and Nellie saw something in it. Confidence. This was a man who was sure of himself. She found herself attracted to him.

"Surely, your father told you how beautiful you are," he said as he cocked his head a little.

"Yes." She laughed. "But that's different than hearing it from a stranger."

Just then the door to the stage office was thrown open forcefully. It hit Nellie from behind and propelled her forward. Her shaky legs weren't able to recover and panic spread across her face. The stranger stepped forward and caught her just as she was about to fall. She threw her arms around him for steadiness.

"Oh my!" Nellie cried out in a nervous, embarrassed voice.

"Ma'am." The man's deep voice was low, almost a course whisper as he leaned down to her ear. "I think this makes us more than strangers now." She pushed away from him, but he held courteously to her arm. "Are you sure you're steady, ma'am?"

"Yes, I think so. Yes, I am. Thank you for catching me."

The look in his eyes burned through her. "It was my pleasure, ma'am." He tipped his hat to her again and strode off. She watched him walk for a moment or two, admiring his form and bearing, then she turned. She was afraid he'd glance back and find her watching him.

It wasn't long before Philip and Bethie returned and he guided them to the nearest restaurant at the end of the block.

"Oh, Philip. Oh, oh, Philip," Nellie said with a big grin on her face. "I think I found my future husband. All you have to do is figure out who he is and bring him to me."

They laughed. "Is that all? How much do we have to go on?

And dang, what all happened while we were gone? It couldn't have been more than eight or ten minutes."

Nellie shrugged and gave them a 'what can I say' look. "He's tall and strong and handsome and confident and polite and helpful and—"

"Damn, Nellie," Philip said with a laugh. He looked at Bethie. "How long were we gone?"

Nellie and Bethie both laughed.

"All right, you didn't get his name?" Philip asked.

"No, but he wore a black hat, the kind a lot of cowboys wear. He'd been somewhere on a trip by himself, riding a horse. He has dark hair, almost black, and deep brown eyes. The kind of eyes that see more than you want them to."

"I don't know what that means," Philip said.

"I do," Bethie said. "I thought you had that kind of eyes when I first met you. I felt like you could read my mind."

He winked at her. "I could."

"Yes, that's it," Nellie said. "Like he could read my mind."

"How would I write that up in an advertisement? In search of handsome, tall, strong, polite, helpful man who can read Nellie's mind."

"Oh, I know it's not enough for you to find him, but that's all I have to go on. I wish we would meet up again. I'm afraid every other man is going to pale in comparison to my handsome stranger," she said wistfully.

"Don't worry too much. There are enough good men in Big Rock to take your mind off him," Bethie offered.

Philip held the door open and the two women walked into the restaurant foyer in front of him. Nellie let out an audible gasp and fought to regain her composure. *It's him!*

"It's him," she whispered to Bethie, trying to be nonchalant, hoping it wasn't obvious that her lips moved and she said anything.

"Philip, come join me. It's a table for four and I'm all by myself," the man said.

"Wes, good to see you," Philip said.

Nellie's eyes widened. *Is this the Wes they've been talking about? My possible best match?* Suddenly, her heart quickened and she wasn't at all sure of herself.

"We will join you, thanks," Philip said.

Wes' eyes didn't leave Nellie's as he stood to pull out a chair for her. At that display of chivalry, Philip pulled out Bethie's chair, too.

"Nellie, this is Wes Hollicker. He's a rancher in Big Rock. Wes, I'd like you to meet Miss Nellie Lancaster."

Wes nodded to Nellie as if tipping his hat. "Hello again, Miss Nellie. This definitely means we aren't strangers anymore."

"It's nice to meet you, Mr. Hollicker."

"Miss Nellie and I sort of met briefly in front of the station office a bit earlier."

Nellie smiled at Philip and Bethie nervously.

*Oh no, that Ladies' Aid woman's been speaking to all the eligible men about me. What did she share with them? What must he think of me? That I have to move to a new town to find a husband, one who's never met me? Oh, no, no, no. No! This is what it'll be like meeting every one of those men! Hold your head up. Smile. You can do this.*

"I just sat down and haven't even ordered yet," Wes said. "Let this be my treat. I assume you wouldn't be here if you weren't planning to catch the stage. It'll be a pleasure to have friends riding it with me."

"Now, Wes," Bethie said with a grin, "something tells me you don't stay strangers with people for very long."

"The last time I took a stagecoach, it was filled with old codgers who complained at every bump. Do you have any idea how many bumps there are when you're riding in a coach? Let me revel in this. I get to enjoy the company of two beautiful ladies and a good friend."

"Nellie," Bethie said with a teasing grin, "this man's a charmer. You'd better look out."

Nellie smiled at them both, hoping it was a confident smile. "I'll certainly be on my guard."

Philip changed the subject. "What's brought you here, Wes? What have you been doing?"

"I went up to Cadron Springs to look at those bulls you told me about. Bought two of them. They'll bring them down next month. Then I had some local business to take care of. I was so upset yesterday when I didn't get my meeting finished in time to catch yesterday's stage. Now I'm glad it worked out this way. Must have been divine intervention." He looked at Nellie again and smiled at her.

*Oh, I am going to have to be on my guard. This man could charm me right out of my bloo—*

Bethie interrupted her thoughts as she picked up the menu. "Nellie, what are you going to order? Everything I've eaten here has been good. Oh, Philip, remember how good those muffins were? Let's see if they'll make a batch for us to take on the stage."

"Good idea. Are you all about ready to order? I'll get her attention," Philip said.

They made their food orders and got their drinks before they even tried to have any more conversation.

"You know, if you build up your herd like you want to, you'll need another couple of bulls before long."

"I know, but I'm afraid of biting off more than I can chew just yet. I'll have to hire some hands pretty soon. It's just about more than I can handle right now."

"Is the bunkhouse finished?"

"It is. Finished and furnished," Wes replied.

"I don't know much about cattle. How many bulls do you need?" Nellie asked. Her eyes showed just a hint of panic, then she calmed when no one reminded her that she grew up on a ranch and if she'd paid attention to anything but herself, she'd know a lot more.

"A rough estimate is about one bull for fifteen to twenty-five cows, depending on the breed," Philip said.

"I knew next to nothing when I first decided to move to Big Rock. Philip and my cousin-in-law Jake have taught me just about everything I know. Is a cousin-in-law a real thing?" He looked at Nellie curiously and she ate it up. "Jake and my cousin Ruby have the ranch next to mine. She's my only relative and I moved here to be near her. I like it here."

"It must be nice having a relative nearby. I don't have any relatives left," Nellie said then instantly regretted it. She hoped they didn't detect any resentment or bitterness in her voice. They all carried on normally, so it must have been taken as an innocent comment.

"Well, I tell you what," Wes said. "I'll take you out to my ranch and show you around it. Maybe I can teach you something about the cattle business in the process."

"What a wonderful idea," Bethie said. Nellie was a little surprised that Bethie seemed to be in favor of her going some-where with Wes unchaperoned. *Is that her plan? To compromise me so I'll have to marry Wes? No, surely not. That's not like Bethie.*

*What about the other men in Big Rock? What if I don't like them after meeting Wes? What if none of them are... are like Wes? Should I try to charm him enough to seal the deal before we even get to town? Oh, Nellie, Nellie. You've never been around men, remember? They never want your company. What should I do? Here's one who seems to enjoy my company. Of course, we just met. I could still mess this up. Just don't say rude things and don't act rudely. It can't be that hard. Other people do it.*

At the end of the meal, they walked back to the stagecoach office together. The women found the stage office's outhouse while the men made sure their luggage was all on board.

"Do you still think he's the one?" Bethie asked as they took care of business. It was, after all, a two-holer.

"I'm so embarrassed now that I said those things about him. But I like him. I mean, so far. I really do." She grinned.

"Don't be embarrassed," Bethie said with a laugh. "I'm glad you like him. He's the one I picked for you in my own mind. I like him, too. I think he's a good man. Philip's done quite a bit of business with him, and he knows him even better than I do."

"Is it foolish of me to want to meet the others anyway? I'm almost afraid to get close to Wes because there might be someone I'll like better. That sounds shallow, doesn't it?"

"Not when we're talking about marriage. It's not something to be taken lightly. There's a quality about his personality and yours, I don't know, you seem to mesh together nicely."

"I sure feel grateful that he missed the stage yesterday," Nellie said and cut her eyes over to Bethie with mischief in them.

"If he did. I find myself wondering if he didn't plan it that way. Derek knew we'd be on this stage. Derek might have told him."

Nellie's mouth opened wide, then closed, pleased that he might have engineered this encounter just to meet her before the other men had a chance. "Do you think?"

Bethie shrugged. "It's possible. But we'll be on that coach for most of two days. That's a good bit of time, probably enough to decide if you like the man or not."

Nellie slowly nodded in agreement.

They were lucky in that there were only six people on the stage. Normally, there were several more, enough so that some men had to ride on top with the luggage. There were two full benches facing each other and a bench in the middle that didn't have a backrest. It was most uncomfortable for a long ride. Nellie was glad no one would have to sit on it. She was particularly glad she wouldn't have to sit on it.

The other two people were a lively middle-aged couple traveling through, so they'd be on the stage for two more days. They all made introductions before boarding the coach.

Philip jumped up into the coach while Wes stayed on the ground to help the ladies negotiate the meager steps. Once they were on the top step, Philip steadied them. Mrs. Crow commented that she'd never had such nice assistance before.

"You young men better stop that or I'm going to have to start being nicer to my wife," Mr. Crow said, garnering chuckles all around. "I don't want her to get used to this."

"Now, Mr. Crow, you don't look like you have a mean bone in your body," Bethie said.

"He doesn't," Mrs. Crow said. "But he doesn't look like it because of those dimples. Sometimes when he needs to be stern, he has to practice looking mean. It's hard for him, but true to his character. Our girls had him wrapped around their little fingers."

"Wanda, you don't have to tell everything you know," he said as he tried several expressions, trying to find one that looked serious. He had the whole group laughing.

Wes sat directly across from Nellie and she wondered if he'd done any maneuvering to make that happen. If he did, he was very slick about it.

The men mostly kept the conversation going about business and politics and they found they had much in common. Mr. Crow had grown up on a ranch, but left when he went off to college and never looked back. He much preferred his career in law, but he had fond memories of his youth on the ranch. His folks had passed away several years ago and he liquidated the property assets and purchased properties in town. He'd been quite successful.

When they found out Mrs. Crow was originally from near Baltimore, Bethie grew excited.

"I'm from there, too! Later we can talk about exactly where we're each from. Wouldn't it be fun if we know some of the same people or have been to the same places?"

"Indeed it would. What brought you out west, dear?"

"My parents. My father had to come out here on business for an indefinite period, so Mother and I came with him. On the train I met a young woman named Molly who was coming to meet—and marry—a man named Derek. As it happened, Molly was Philip's cousin and Derek was Philip's good friend."

Philip laughed. "I introduced the two of them. By mail. And they ended up writing to each other and getting married. They both were widowed at very young ages and I just knew they had to end up together. And we all ended up in Big Rock."

"What a wonderful story," Mrs. Crow said. "Now Big Rock, isn't that the place for mail order brides? I believe I read a newspaper article about it. Maybe it was in a periodical."

"Yes, ma'am, that's us, all right. Our town grew so fast, we knew we had to get women to move here to keep the men in town and keep businesses open," Bethie said.

Nellie started to flush in anticipation, afraid they would ask her if she was a mail order bride. *How am I going to answer that? It'll be doubly hard in front of Wes. Maybe we don't have to say anything. We didn't mention anything about me, really. They probably assume I already live there. Deep breath. It'll be fine. I'll be fine.*

"Mr. Hollicker, what do you do for a living in Big Rock?" Mrs. Crow asked politely.

"Please call me Wes, ma'am. I have a little ranch just outside of town. I've only had it a year or so. Before that I grew up in Dodge's Summit and then went to college. Not too long after college, my mother passed away and I discovered I had a cousin I'd never known about. I set about finding her, and I finally did find her in Big Rock. Now I have a ranch right next to theirs."

Mrs. Crow clasped her hands together excitedly. "Another wonderful story! My, I do get the feeling Big Rock has a rich history in all its people. I do enjoy learning about people and how they've settled out here. It's fascinating, don't you think?"

Mr. Crow leaned back, pushing against the back of his seat

and stretching out his legs. "That, my friends, is my wife's way of admitting she's nosey." His dimpled grin belied what could have been construed as a criticism.

Mrs. Crow leaned into him affectionately. "Oh, you," she said as she blew him a kiss. "You know you love to hear stories like this, too."

He laughed. "She's right. I do."

Nellie watched the older couple enjoy themselves. She paid attention to their mannerisms and noticed some similarities with the way Philip and Bethie acted when they were together. They touched each other. Not enough to be offensive to others, but a touch here and there. They smiled at each other. *Is it my imagination or can I imagine Mother and Daddy being like that with each other? I remember them hugging and kissing in the mornings after breakfast before he left for the barn. I remember they patted each other. I remember little kisses here and there. They hugged and patted and kissed me, too, but it was different somehow with a child. That's love. That's the love I want with a man. Is Wes the man? The way he moves, the way he seems so comfortable in his own skin, I can see wanting to reach over and pat his arm or his leg…*

"Nellie, do you enjoy reading?" Mrs. Crow asked for the second time.

"Oh, I'm sorry," Nellie said, red-faced. "I'm afraid I let my mind wander."

Nellie felt Wes' eyes on her and couldn't keep herself from looking at him. He had a little grin on his face, sort of a smirk, like he'd caught her doing something wrong and now they shared a secret he could hold over her.

She cleared her throat and turned back to Mrs. Crow. "Lately, I've enjoyed reading the works of Mark Twain."

"Oh, yes, we've read them a time or two. They're delightful. Sometimes Mr. Crow reads aloud in the evenings while I knit."

Did she call him Mr. Crow because they were among relative

strangers, she wondered, or does she always call her husband Mr. Crow? Surely not.

"Mrs. Hickam, do you enjoy reading?"

"I do some," Bethie said. "I have to admit, I enjoy reading romantic novels. Sometimes Philip makes fun of me for it."

"I don't make fun of you," he said. "I simply keep saying I need to build more bookcases for them."

Nellie saw Bethie smile at Philip and pat his arm.

*Yes, that's definitely what I want. Touches. Shared memories. Shared secrets.*

Before long they came to the first rest stop where they'd get fresh horses. Wes was the first one down and he helped all three ladies step down.

The driver announced that this stop had no convenience facilities and they'd have to relieve themselves behind the bushes. "Ladies usually choose that cluster of bushes over there." He pointed and the three women took off in that direction.

Since they weren't alone, Nellie didn't want to bring up the subject of Wes with Bethie. Maybe there would be time later. As they walked back toward the wagon, the driver and the swing stationmaster were finishing with the horses. Mr. Crow was nowhere in sight. Philip and Wes seemed engaged in a deep discussion that ended with big smiles, a handshake, and Philip slapping Wes' shoulder as if in congratulations. What could that be about? When they turned back toward the wagon, Wes' eyes met hers and his grin broadened. He acknowledged her with a nod and she smiled back at him.

Before they got back on the coach, the driver asked if any of them needed their canteens refilled from the keg on the back of the coach. They didn't, but Bethie said she'd never heard a driver ask that before. It was a nice touch, she said, having him see to their needs.

Once back onboard, Nellie suggested it might be nice to share the muffins they had. Bethie agreed and pulled out the bag from the restaurant. They were individually wrapped in newspaper so Bethie handed two of them to Mr. and Mrs. Crow.

"Oh, my, dear, these are large muffins. Mr. Crow and I can share one of them. We're at that age, you know, having to watch our waistlines."

Philip laughed. "Nonsense. Besides, when you taste these, you'll want the whole bag to yourself."

They ended up all eating a whole one each and the ladies all tried to identify the flavors. They knew cinnamon and clove were two ingredients, but they couldn't all three agree that nutmeg was included. Or was it allspice?

Recipes were the dominant topic of conversation until the next stop, and at one point Nellie pointed out quietly that all three men had their heads leaned back or leaned to the side with their eyes closed. For some reason, they were all three most amused by it.

The next stop boasted an outhouse, such as it was. The gentlemen let the ladies go first, but Wes and Mr. Crow didn't want to wait. One found a large tree to hide behind and the other went behind the lean-to barn.

Again, Wes and Philip helped the ladies step up into the coach. Mrs. Crow was first because she always sat by the far window seat. Next was Bethie, then Nellie, because Nellie sat by the window seat nearest the door.

Nellie wondered if it was her imagination or if Wes held her just a bit more intimately this time, more so than he did with the others. The other times when he'd helped her, and when he helped the other ladies this time, he simply took their hand to help steady them. He didn't do that with her this time. No, he put one hand around her forearm and the other one on the small of her back, applying just a little pressure. The small of her back! That was definitely more intimate. The memory of his touch on her lingered after he removed his hands.

As she sat, she watched him step up into the coach and close the door. He leaned over her and knocked on the wall behind her to let the driver know they were all inside and ready. As he sat, his eyes found hers and the look on his face was, was... was what? A smile? A smirk? No, she decided it wasn't a bad thing. There wasn't any indication he thought he went over the line and there wasn't any hint of smugness, as though he thought he'd gotten away with something. No, it was a good thing. A shared secret! Her heart skipped a beat and she hoped he wasn't playing with her emotions. She didn't think he would, based on Philip and Bethie's opinions of him.

*A shared secret.* She liked that thought. Maybe it was her imagination, maybe not. She liked to think not. *If it feels this good to have such a tiny secret, think how it must feel to share big ones. To share the memory of intimacy, for example. Yes, I'm going to like that a lot.*

Philip let them know there would be one more stop to change horses, then the stop after that would be at Cooper's Gap where their supper would be provided and they'd spend the night. Nellie wondered if there might be an opportunity to be alone with Wes for a few minutes. She didn't know what she'd do with those few minutes, but she wanted them, nonetheless.

There was a lull in the conversation and Mrs. Crow piped up, "Would anyone enjoy playing a word game with me? I find them an enjoyable way to pass time."

"I will," Bethie said, then Nellie said she'd like to, too. Finally, the men agreed to play as well.

"All right then. We can start with Mr. Hickam, and he'll say a type of animal. Then the next person chooses an animal that begins with the last letter of what he said. For example, if we were doing places, I might say Omaha, then the next person might say Alabama. Ready?"

She motioned toward Philip. "You start."

"Snake," Philip said.

Bethie wasted no time. "Elephant."

Neither did Nellie. "Tiger."

Wes was quick, too. "Rhino."

Mr. Crow started to say something, then he stopped and looked at Wes. "Should I go for an O or an S?"

Wes shrugged. "Your choice."

Mr. Crow shrugged back. "Otter."

Mrs. Crow slowly mentioned her choice of animals. "Reindeer."

There were some *aahs* and Bethie giggled.

Philip jumped back in. "Rooster."

"Roadrunner."

"Rabbit."

"Toad."

"Dolphin."

"Nightingale," Mrs. Crow chipped in.

"Eagle."

Bethie got a mischievous look on her face and said, "Emu."

Nellie's shoulders slumped. "And I was doing so well. Really? U?" She looked at Bethie scornfully and Bethie's giggles turned into a full-fledged laugh.

"Give up yet?" Bethie asked.

"No, just give me a minute," she said, a rueful smirk across her face. Suddenly, she brightened and nearly jumped up with excitement. "Urchin! A sea urchin!"

A couple of others laughed at her excitement. Wes looked at her and chuckled. "I would have just said ugly emu."

That brought laughs from everyone and from then on when the player couldn't think of an appropriately named animal, they just stuck on an adjective that started with the correct letter. And more often than not, it was an emu. Ugly emu. Yellow emu. Tall emu. Smug emu. Rabid emu. Educated emu. Frustrated emu.

That got them almost all the way to the next swing station stop where they'd get fresh horses again.

When they stopped, Wes took special care to not only take

Nellie's hand to help her down, but he put his hand on her upper arm, too. Once down, she turned to watch and he didn't do that with the other ladies. *So it was just for me.*

This stop took a little longer, something about one of the horses throwing a shoe, whatever that meant. She hadn't completely understood the words the driver grumbled. Nellie was standing with the other two ladies when Wes came up beside her and put his hand on her shoulder.

"Will you walk with me?" he asked. He smiled at Bethie and promised to stay close.

When they'd stepped a few feet away, he began, "Nellie, I waited until after I talked to Philip about it to say anything to you, but I would like to call on you. Court you if that's all right."

*It's happening.*

"Oh, my," she said as she struggled for words. "Is that what you were talking so seriously about with Philip earlier?"

He grinned. "Yes. My message to him might have been a little stronger."

"I don't understand," she said.

"I told him I'm going to marry you."

She stopped walking and gasped, a shocked expression on her face. "You did?"

"I did. I told him I'd like to court you if you didn't agree to marry me right off."

"What if I decide not to marry you at all?"

"I'm a gentleman, Nellie. I'll back off and wish the best to the next man."

"You'd let me go that easily?" she asked, feeling bold enough to tease him a little.

"No, I don't plan to let you go at all. You'll marry me."

He pulled her behind a big tree out of sight of the others. And he kissed her.

It was nothing like she expected and it was everything she expected, and more. His lips were tender, slowly pressing into hers, compelling her to press back. He nipped at her lips and she felt his hand at the back of her head, making it clear he didn't wish the kiss to end, either. His lips sucked her lower one in and he teased it with his tongue. Then he went back to a full on kiss and this time his tongue teased her tongue. She felt it all the way to her womanly core.

He pulled away but still held the back of her head. "I want you to be my wife, Nellie."

"I don't know what to say, Wes, this is so soon. You just met me today!"

"But I've been thinking about you ever since Harriet Smithers mentioned you to me."

A pall descended on her and Nellie felt like she shrunk a little. "That's the Ladies' Aid lady, isn't it? How could you possibly want me after learning all those bad things about me?"

He chuckled. "Well, we all have our faults. I didn't think there was anything in your father's letter that couldn't be overcome."

Nellie screwed up her face. "You read the letter?"

"I did. It's clear your father loved you very much and wanted what's best for you. His love for you shone through in that letter. That part was touching, sweet. And maybe an insight into why he let you run wild. Maybe that's the part that charmed me, I don't know. But I knew when I read it that I had to know more about you. Now that I've been around you, I know all I need to know. I want to marry you. And soon."

"But all those things he said about me? That I was spoiled and I can be rude and condescending?"

"You haven't been at all that way today, have you?"

"Well, no," she said.

"Then look on the bright side. You don't have to hide anything from me because I already know your bad traits."

Nellie had to laugh at that.

"Tell me this. Is it possible you'll say yes?" Wes asked.

"Of course, it's possible, but—"

"That's all I need to know."

He kissed her again but pulled her closer to him. Nellie relished the feel of the hug, of his strong arms around her. It made her feel wanted, desired, needed, and safe. She would wonder later if *safe* was what affected her the most.

The walk back to the stage was slow and Nellie wondered if the others could tell by looking at her what had happened. Probably not the men, but maybe the women. Women's intuition, or something like that. Could Bethie know by looking at her that she'd been kissed? Could her eyes give it away? Maybe a certain softness to them? Or a softness in the way she held her mouth? Could they see that Wes walked closer to her than he did before, or that he seemed to touch her just a little more than was necessary?

*The touching.* They might just seem like innocent touches if observed by a stranger. He took her elbow or gently nudged her shoulder. The touch on her back might have seemed perfectly normal to anyone else, but only she felt the small, caressing circles he drew on her with his fingers. *Yes, this is how Philip and Bethie act with each other and the Crows, too.*

The soft smile on Nellie's face widened as she felt Wes' eyes on her and she looked up to meet them.

When the stage got underway, it was Philip who spoke up first. "Well, Mrs. Crow, do you have any games for this last leg of today's journey? We all enjoyed that last one."

She laughed. "I do, but I'm afraid my brain's already been stretched to its limit for the day. But I have another idea. You travel through here quite a bit. Why don't you tell us what to expect at Cooper's Gap?"

Philip nodded and chuckled. "The Coopers are nice; you'll like them. Not very much to the place, really. The best thing about it is the food. Mrs. Cooper and her daughters do a fine job with that. The worst thing for me," he said as he reached for Bethie's hand, "is that the sleeping is dormitory style. One room for the men and another for the women. And they must have put the nice beds in the ladies' room because the cots in the men's room are dreadful."

"Then they must have saved the nice beds for the family, because we have dreadful cots, too," Bethie chimed in.

Philip grinned at her and continued. "Their barn is bigger than you'd expect for a house that size, but it's because they're a changing station for stage teams, too, just like all the other stops we had today."

Nellie only caught parts of the conversation. Her thoughts and her eyes were mostly on Wes, whose eyes held hers with a tenderness her heart responded to. Sometimes her eyes dropped down to his lips and the memory of their kisses gave her a response somewhat lower than her heart.

They had a secret. The delicious thought of that delighted Nellie's sense of romance. For now, it was a big secret, a very big one. She didn't know how long she'd be able to keep it from Bethie, whether her friend guessed it, or whether she couldn't hold it anymore and went running to her to share it.

The conversation that ensued in the coach centered on the best foods each had eaten and where they'd eaten it, and even exotic foods from other continents, but Nellie only participated as much as she had to for the sake of etiquette. She had much bigger and more exciting things on her mind.

Mrs. Cooper went out to meet the coach riders as they disembarked. Despite that, Nellie still bestowed upon Wes the sweetest smile as she stepped down and he returned it. She didn't even care if Mrs. Cooper noticed.

Introductions were made and their hostess explained that they might want to go around to the back to refresh themselves and that they'd find water and cloths on the back porch to wash their faces and hands before supper. The ladies took off immediately. The men knew they'd have to wait anyway, so they stood around chatting and stretching for a few minutes to kill time.

The long dining table was not only long, but extra wide. Philip had been right; it was laden with delicious food. As the meal wound down and they were all enjoying butter cookies for dessert, Mrs. Cooper asked Bethie if she would mind entertaining them for a few minutes before they all retired.

Bethie brightened and said she'd be delighted to. Nellie had heard her humming a few times and singing under her breath, so she knew she must love to sing.

Nellie chose to sit on a loveseat made for two people to occupy. She was most gratified when Wes wasted no time getting to her and sitting by her side. He sat very close. *He must have been watching me.*

Mrs. Cooper left her girls to clean up and joined the guests in the big parlor. Mr. Cooper picked up his guitar and began to play "Aura Lee." Bethie stood by the fireplace and smiled at him; apparently it was his favorite song.

When she began to sing, the others couldn't help but stop to listen. Nellie even saw the girls peek around the corner of the kitchen to listen. It was as though Bethie cast a charm when she sang. It would have been obvious that the first few songs were Mr. Cooper's favorites even if he hadn't told everyone. After those were performed, there were a few requests by the listeners, even one or two from the girls still cleaning the kitchen. Bethie knew all the songs, even the ones Mr. Cooper didn't know. At one point, and to everyone's surprise, she called Philip to join her and they sang a couple of duets. She finished by singing two sweet lullabies to help calm everyone before retiring.

As she lay in her cot, Nellie tossed and turned. *Shall I marry him? I like him, I like him a lot. Do I love him? I only just met him! How could it be love? Does it have to be love already? I know of arranged marriages where couples never even met before marrying, and they ended up in love with very happy unions. Could Wes and I be like that? We're attracted to each other, that's undeniable, but that's not the same as love. Can a deep and abiding love grow from what we have now? It could happen, couldn't it? But what if I mess it up? What if I get out on his ranch and grow bored with it? What if my physical attraction to Wes isn't enough to keep my rudeness and brattiness from popping up? What if I decide I don't like him very much after all? It might be different when I have to cook every day and keep up with the chores, and then he'll come in all dirty from being with cows and horses all day. He'll be dirty and sweaty. Then I'll have to clean up after him... Oh, no, that's not romantic at all. How can love grow in that kind of atmosphere? But it has for other people. What if he expects too much of me? What if I can't cook and clean and run his household as well as he likes? Will he be patient? Will he get upset with me? Upset with me—oh no—what will he do when he's upset with me?*

Her thoughts went back to that first day that Bethie and Philip came and her father insisted that Philip belt her. Would Wes handle her that way? Bethie seemed to think it was no big deal, and that it happened to a lot of people. *But I'm not like a lot of people!*

Nellie heard the soft, rhythmic sound of Mrs. Crow's heavy breathing. It was actually a nice sound, a little more than a normal breath but not quite a snore, either. Any other time, it might have lulled her to sleep.

She quietly sat up and lit the candle on the little nightstand next to her cot and put the glass chimney over it.

"Bethie," she whispered as she gently shook her shoulder. "Go to the outhouse with me."

"All right," Bethie answered and Nellie could see that her eyes were still closed even as she sat up.

They put on their shoes but didn't fasten them and picked up the quilts from their cots to wrap around themselves. Outside, almost to the outhouse, Nellie stopped and turned to her friend.

"First, I want to know if you'll sing at my wedding."

"Of course, I will," she said. "I would have offered even if you didn't ask. We have plenty of time to decide... wait."

The look on Nellie's face made her stop mid-sentence. "Nellie, is there something you want to tell me?"

"Of course, there is," Nellie answered with a laugh. "Did you think I really needed to use the outhouse? He asked me today, at the last stop before this one."

Bethie could barely contain herself; she jumped up and down a little. Nellie would have, too, if she hadn't been holding the candle with a glass chimney.

"How did he do it? What did he say?"

"He said he had waited to get Philip's blessing to court me. Actually, he told Philip he was going to marry me. He told me that, too. And he kissed me. Twice. Oh, Bethie, I thought it was so romantic."

"Well, what did you say?"

"That it was so soon and he couldn't know. But he said he did know. He read Daddy's letter and wasn't scared off by it. Instead, he wanted to meet me even more. He said he would court me if I wasn't ready to say yes yet. I asked him what he'd do if I said I wouldn't marry him."

"And?"

"He said he's a gentleman and he'd graciously bow out. I teased him a little and asked him if he'd give up so easily. He said he wouldn't have to give up, that I'll marry him."

"Will you?"

"It's looking very promising. But I still have so many questions, Bethie! What if I'm not a good enough cook? Or I don't keep house like he likes? Or I get tired of living on a ranch and feel trapped? What if he gets angry with me about something? What if that daily grind of working all day takes its toll on me? You know I've worked, but not as much as a rancher's wife probably has to. What if there's something about me he doesn't like?"

"I'm a rancher's wife, you know. Philip is more successful than most, I grant you that, but our life is wonderful. Wes has the wherewithal to give you the kind of life I lead. It's not bad at all. I cook and I clean, but we have help with some things. I wouldn't trade my life for anything."

"Really?"

"Absolutely. There's only one way you can calm your mind about these things. All those questions and what-ifs you just asked me? Ask Wes the same questions. Let him know what you're concerned about."

"All right. I should be able to talk to him about those things, right? They're reasonable questions for a fiancée, aren't they?"

"They certainly are. Are you ready to go back in now? It's getting cool."

"Yes."

"Wait." Bethie stood for a split second then turned. "No, I'd better use this while I can."

Nellie sighed. "Me, too. You can hold the candle while I'm in there."

THE EXCITEMENT MOUNTED as the stage neared Big Rock. They knew Derek would be waiting with the wagon but they didn't know if Molly and the children would be with him. Wes had wired Jake so he hoped both Jake and Ruby would be there so they could meet Nellie.

When they stopped and Wes opened the coach door, the first person he saw was Ruby. He stepped down and quickly kissed his cousin on the cheek before turning back to help Nellie step down.

"Help them down, will you, Jake?" he called over his shoulder as he guided his two favorite women to a spot out of the way.

"Nellie, this is my cousin, Ruby Jernigan. And Ruby, this is Nellie Lancaster."

Nellie's smile was genuine. "Ruby, I've heard so much about you. Wes talks about you and Jake fondly."

"Ruby, I've asked Nellie to marry me. Maybe you can help me give her the nudge she needs to finally say yes."

Nellie grinned, a little embarrassed, and Ruby said, "Now, cousin, if you can't persuade her on your own, maybe you don't deserve her."

That drew chuckles from Nellie and put her at ease immediately with Ruby. Wes' arm was around her waist and she loved the possessive and protective feeling that gave her. And the touch.

Derek and Molly were there, too, along with Philip and Bethie's two boys and their own son and daughter. When they were introduced, Nellie found herself trying to remember their names even more than the adults' names.

Wes' meager bags were loaded on Jake's buggy, and the wagon was nearly filled with the other's things. They loaded it carefully, knowing they'd need to fit two adults and four children back there, too.

All headed to Mary's Restaurant where the grownups found a table that would accommodate the eight of them, while a smaller table next to it would fit the children. Wes was quick to pull out a chair for Nellie and he put his hand on her shoulder for an instant before he sat next to her. Bethie and Molly both giggled under their breath when their husbands, after seeing Wes do that, pulled out their chairs.

Conversation was light as everyone was eager to get home, Nellie doubly eager to get to a home she'd never even seen. She couldn't imagine their place being big enough to contain all the things she'd shipped.

Wes was just a little extra solicitous of her as they ate. He asked if she wanted her drink refilled, made sure the condiments were within her reach, and occasionally rested his arm on the back of her chair for a moment or two. What the others couldn't see was that once in a while his hand disappeared under the table and he patted her leg. Neither of them reacted and she thought it was another delectable and slightly sinful secret.

After the meal they all said their goodbyes to the Crows, who promised to write. Jake and Ruby again told Nellie how happy they were she was there. When he couldn't stay any longer without detaining the others, Wes put a hand on either side of her waist and leaned down to kiss her forehead, then her cheek. He whispered, "In my mind I'm kissing your lips and holding you close to me."

She blushed a little, then reminded him to come the next evening for dinner.

The men allowed the women to sit on the wagon seat for the ride home, which meant that Molly took the reins and Nellie sat between her and Bethie. Philip sat just behind Bethie, his long legs spread out nearly to the other side of the wagon. Derek sat similarly, facing Philip. The children all sat on the tailgate with their feet dangling off, lost in their own play world.

"I think I'm going to like this town," Nellie said. "It's smaller than home, but the people are nice. How long is the drive to the ranch?"

"About an hour, maybe a little more."

"Where does Wes live?"

Philip answered, "He lives about thirty-five minutes on the other side of town."

"Oh, that'll take a long time for him to visit. Why, he'll be on the road for over three hours just to come see me. That's a long time."

"I'm pretty sure he thinks you're worth it," Bethie said.

"Well now, who are some of the other men in town?"

"Oh, Nellie, I'm afraid there won't be any other men for you now," Molly said.

"Really? Why not? I thought I'd be meeting several potential husbands. I mean, I think I've settled on Wes, but it might be nice to meet some others."

"'Fraid not, Nell," Philip said. "Nobody else is going to be calling."

"I'm confused. I thought you had a whole town full of single men for me to meet."

"We do," Molly said, "but it's a small town and word's probably out all over it now about you and Wes."

Nellie looked at Molly, perplexed. "Philip, is that true?" she asked, still looking at Molly.

"Yes, ma'am, it is."

"Uh hum," Derek agreed.

Molly explained, "Nellie, you know how dogs mark their territory so other dogs won't encroach?"

"Yes," she answered slowly.

Bethie finished, "Well, Wes might as well have peed all over you."

"She's right," Philip said. "The other men in town will respect what Wes already has with you. They'll stay away."

"Well," Nellie said. "I guess it's safe for me to tell Wes I'll marry him, then. Otherwise, I won't be any better off than I was before." She sounded a little resigned to her fate.

"You aren't really disappointed, are you? Last night you were excited," Bethie reminded her.

Nellie smiled at the memory. "No, I'm not disappointed. Deep down I knew I was going to tell him yes. I wanted to make him work for it a little more, though," she said with a laugh.

A chuckle came from behind her. It was a deep voice and she knew it was Derek speaking. "Nothing says you have to make it easy for him. You can still make him work for it. We won't tell."

"You aren't going to string him along, are you?" That was Bethie.

"No, but he did say he was willing to court me if I don't say yes immediately. I could just let him court me."

"You could, but remember he has a ranch and it's a good three hour round trip to our place," Philip said.

"Oh, right," Nellie said. "I'll remember that. He probably won't be able to come that often."

Molly slowed the team of horses. "Bumpy patch coming up. We had a storm that washed out holes all across the road." She raised her voice to be heard. "You young'uns hold on!"

The front wheels dipped and the wagon wobbled until the back wheels reached the ruts. The wobbling momentum and the dip caused the back of the wagon to bounce. Six-year-old Jason was tossed up and landed sprawled out on the road.

"Lost one!" Derek called out to Molly. Jason was one of their two.

"I'm all right!" Jason called out but stayed where he was.

Molly *whoaed* the horses to a stop. Seven year old Rosemary jumped down to help her brother back up, then she sat with her arm around him when they were settled again. "I'll hold you," she assured him.

Derek thought that was touching enough that he reached up and got Molly's attention so she could see them.

Nellie saw that exchange and wondered about having children with Wes. She'd always been so self-centered, she'd never considered having them. Wes was the kind of man who'd want children, she thought. A sense of unease came over her. *Oh great, that's even more work. Now I'll have cooking, cleaning, and babies to take care of. What if I'm not good with babies? I've never been around them. Wes is going to be so disappointed in me. I'm just not prepared for this! What if I'm a bad mother? I don't know anything about taking care of them. What if I do something wrong?*

*I need to talk to Bethie about all these things. No, no, she was right last night. I need to talk to Wes about these things. When we get to Bethie's, I'll make a list of my concerns after I unpack.*

When they came to the Hickam Ranch, Nellie was pleasantly surprised by how large and beautiful it was. The home was one of the biggest she'd ever seen. It had a huge porch that wrapped around three sides and she saw toys put away against the house.

It occurred to her that the children could still play outside when it rained. Not that it rained that much in Wyoming, but still, it was a nice concept. There were groupings of porch swings and rocking chairs and tables. There was a flower garden in front of the porch that spanned two sides of the house. The front steps were wide, so wide that a handrail was placed down the middle. The windows all had shutters and the upstairs windows had window boxes for flowers. Nellie figured there were no flower boxes on the downstairs windows because the sun couldn't reach them.

There was a guesthouse to the back and side of the big house. Bethie explained that Philip built it for her parents while she was expecting their first child. They visited for two or three months at a time but were away right now.

There were two huge barns, each beautiful in its own right. Nellie figured that was because Philip made his living with live-stock, and they probably made quite an impression on his customers who visited.

Bethie had mentioned that Wes had the wherewithal to take good care of Nellie, but she doubted if he could afford anything like this. The Hickam ranch was a showplace.

When the wagon came to a stop, the children all jumped and ran up to the porch to grab something to play with. The men each held on to the side railing and jumped over, landing on their feet. They helped the ladies down and Philip told them to go on inside and show Nellie around while he and Derek unloaded all their things.

"I know you're going to love it here," Molly said. "You might decide not to marry Wes just so you can stay permanently," she said with a laugh. "Everybody loves visiting Philip and Bethie."

Nellie smiled at the thought. From what she knew of them thus far, she could believe it. They were fun to be with, they clearly loved each other, and both seemed to have a friendly and generous spirit. Why, they'd put their whole lives on hold for an indefinite period of time, forcing them to be away from their own home and family, just because her father asked them to help. It struck her at that moment just how much she owed to the Hickams.

Bethie first took Nellie by the hand and led her to her guest suite. "You'll have your own water closet with this room so you won't have to share. It's small, but it gets the job done."

"It's beautiful, Bethie. I want you to know how grateful I am to you and Philip for this."

"Well, you aren't a guest here; this isn't a hotel," Bethie said with a laugh, "you're family. I'll tell you the same thing I tell the little ones. I expect you to clean up after yourself."

Nellie chuckled at that and promised to do so. She went over to the window and opened it. "It's just so beautiful here! Oh, look, you even have a gazebo out back. It's lovely. Molly's right, I might decide to stay."

Molly snickered behind them. "I suppose Wes could move in, too; the place is big enough."

"Well," Bethie said, "if he does, he's cleaning up after himself."

THE EVENING PROVED to be short and they all retired early, even the children. As Nellie lay in bed, she thought of all the worries and questions she had spinning in her head. She turned on her side, picked up the paper and pencil beside the lamp on the bedside table, and began to write.

QUESTIONS FOR WES:

1. How do you feel about children?

- I've never been around them, don't know how to take care of them

- how many would you like to have?

- what if I'm not a good mother?
2. What if you grow tired of me?
3. What if I grow bored of living on a ranch?
4. What if my bad traits start popping up?
5. What if I don't cook well enough for you?
6. What if I don't keep house well enough to suit you?
- laundry? Please, please no...
7. What if I do something that makes you angry?

*THIS IS GOING to be some serious discussion.*

NELLIE WAS AWAKENED by the sound of laughter from down the hall and decided she'd better get up. She didn't want to appear to be a lazy guest. Once dressed, she headed to the kitchen where she found Bethie already beginning breakfast preparations.

"I have coffee on already. Grab the bacon out of the icebox."

"Oh! You have an icebox. We always wanted one, but Daddy said our cold cellar was almost as cold as one, and it didn't need ice."

"Philip has to send hands up to the snow level on the mountains to bring it back, so we don't always have it on hand. Sure is nice when we do, though."

Nellie got the bacon and pulled out the jar of cream at the same time.

"What do you think, biscuits or toast?"

Nellie responded with a suggestion to fix whatever the little ones would eat.

"Those hungry little mouths would eat dirt if you put it on a plate in front of them. I think biscuits. Biscuits, bacon, jam, jelly, and honey. Does that sound all right with you?"

Nellie agreed and set about slicing the bacon into the thinnest slices she could manage.

~

AFTER BREAKFAST, Nellie found Philip in his office. "Do you have a minute?"

"Of course, I do. Come on in and sit down. What can I do for you?"

"You know Wes is coming over tonight. I was just wondering if, um, you mentioned to him about that first day you and Bethie came to our ranch."

Philip leaned forward on his elbows. "No, Nellie, I didn't. I wouldn't. I think that's your story to tell, not mine."

She sighed in relief then looked at him. "Do you think I should tell him? I mean, would you want to know?"

He leaned back again and considered it. "To tell the truth, I'm not sure I would. From the standpoint of not having any secrets between couples, you could make the argument that you should get it out in the open. But on the other hand, he would know that I saw you, well, you know. He might not like that. And there's the argument that he should get to know you as you are now, not based on things that happened in the past."

Nellie lowered her head, embarrassed. "You realize you aren't helping me decide."

Philip grinned. "Yes, I do know that. It's not an easy question. But that incident was orchestrated by your father and done in front of him, so that should put his mind at ease. I don't believe he'd think I acted improperly."

"I don't think so, either. And that's a good point about it being all Daddy's doing. Surely, that would make it easier for him to take. I think I won't volunteer anything until the subject comes up and it seems like I should tell him."

"Good idea. Just don't lie to him. That never goes well," Philip said.

~

LATE THAT AFTERNOON Nellie pulled her pies out of the oven and decided to sit out front on a swing to wait for Wes. *She pulled her discussion list out of her pocket and shook her head at it. Am I being silly? Am I not being worried enough? Even though everyone says Wes is a good man, a kind man, how can I be sure? Maybe all those people just haven't seen an angry side of him. Maybe they haven't been around him in those types of circumstances where he might blow up and lose his temper. How can I know? How can I be sure?*

She didn't have to wait much longer before she saw Wes on his horse galloping toward her. She stepped down on the lowest front step. Nellie wondered why he veered off to the side until she saw him stop at the trough beside an ornate pump handle. He tethered the horse and walked toward her, a big grin on his face.

*That face. The grin, the eyes, those broad shoulders and the muscles everywhere. Oh, the muscles. The muscles that made her feel safe.* She felt some of her doubts vanishing, then reminded herself that even sexy, handsome men can have tempers.

She started to turn and head up the steps but he stopped her. "Our lips are closer to the same level with you on that step," he said with a lazy grin and his eyes on her mouth. Her smile melted in the kiss. It was just one kiss, but it was a good one.

He rested his forehead against hers and held her eyes. "Have you decided to marry me?"

"It's looking promising," Nellie said.

"What can I do to make that 'yes' get here quicker?"

"I have a short list of questions to ask you. Things I'm concerned about and we should talk over before I give you a wholehearted answer."

"Well, let's sit down and I'll answer anything you ask. It's important to me that you go into this confidently. I don't want you to have any lingering doubts. Doubts don't make a good foundation."

"You don't think I'm silly?"

"Of course not."

"I guess I should wait until we discuss these things before I ask that. You might change your mind."

"That could be true. Let's sit down and you can start asking away."

Bethie stepped out on the front porch holding two glasses of iced tea. "Hello, Wes. I heard you ride up. Here's some iced tea for you both. Nellie, why don't you two take these drinks out to the gazebo where you can visit in private. I'll make sure the boys leave you alone. I'll call you in when we're ready to eat."

They thanked her for the tea and got situated in the gazebo before getting down to the serious topics.

Wes gave her his undivided attention. She knew that by the way he leaned forward toward her, his elbows on his thighs. He looked like he'd hang on to her every word.

She set her tea glass down on a side table and pulled out the list from her pocket. "All right, here goes. We haven't talked about children. Do you want them?"

"I would like to have a family with you in time. It's not a strong goal at the moment, but we have to be mindful that a baby might come along at any time. We're both healthy and I expect sexual relations will play a big part in our relationship. I hope you want that, too. Since that's where babies come from, it could happen."

Nellie wasn't sure what she had wanted him to say. She'd been thinking children would be a nuisance but when he said he'd like to have a family with her, she suddenly saw it differently. *We'll be a family. Together.*

Her expression must have softened because he asked, "Was that the right answer?"

"It was a fine one. Do you see us with a large family or a small one?"

"I don't really have a picture in my head, or a preference. I'll be grateful for whatever we're blessed with. I would love to have you to myself for a while, though. There is something I can do to try not to give you a baby just yet, but it doesn't always work."

"There is?"

"How much do you know about marital relations, Nellie?"

"I know next to nothing. My mother died before it was even a topic I'd consider and I could never ask Daddy. I tried to talk to Mrs. Nelson a few times but she dismissed me and told me I didn't need to know those things yet. I didn't need to know them until I got married."

"All right, I understand. That's a topic we can cover in our next big discussion. Right now, I want to cover your list and ease your mind."

"Good idea." She looked at her list and knew the next item would show her insecurity. "I've never been around children before. What if I'm not a good mother?"

"Eve had never been around children before, either," Wes said with a grin. "I imagine throughout history, women who had never been around children have given birth to them. I've never been a father, either, but I'm going to do the best I can to be a good one. You aren't alone, Nellie, I'll be right in there with you. We'll be new parents together. We'll help and support each other."

She smiled. "That was definitely the best answer."

"Good. Next?"

She looked down her list, wanting to hold off on a couple. "I can cook basic things, but I wasn't the main cook at home. I don't have a lot of experience, but there are two or three things I'm good at. What if you don't like my cooking?"

"I don't expect that to be a problem. I'll eat anything. I even have a couple of favorite dishes, and as it happens, I'm pretty good with them. I can help with the cooking. I'll teach you what I do well and you can teach me what you do well. All that matters is that we don't starve. I've been cooking for myself since I moved here, and I can keep doing the cooking if you want. Hell, if it gets bad enough, I'll hire somebody to cook."

Nellie laughed. "Another good answer. For now, it sounds like we can handle it. In the future, though, I think I might keep that option open to hire someone to do some of the cooking."

"If that'll get you to say 'yes' then it's a deal."

She laughed. "It's looking better and better." She looked at her list again. "Whew. Same type thing for this one. My house-keeping skills might leave something to be desired. What if I can't keep house to suit you?"

"That's another easy one. As you can imagine, I've been keeping house myself, and not very well." He laughed. "If you do anything at all to clean, it'll be an improvement. Sometimes Ruby comes to help me. But we can hire someone to come in once or twice a week to help out, maybe the same person can cook, too. I bet we could find someone who lives on that side of town, maybe the wife or daughter of a miner, who would like to make some extra money. They pay well there, but some might want to earn some more. Let's get settled in and see what will work best for us. Oh, laundry. There's a lady in town that does my laundry. I want to keep on using her. She's supporting her family on that money. You didn't have your heart set on washing the clothes and linens, did you?"

That made her laugh out loud, a deep belly laugh. "That was next on my list. I've never had to do any laundry."

This time he laughed out loud. "I guess that's another thing I'll have to teach you. Even though I send most of it to the laundry, I still end up having to do some myself. It's not my favorite thing. Next?"

She checked her list and looked up at him slowly.

"What if you grow tired of me? Maybe decide you were

wrong to want to marry me?"

He took her hands, making her fold up the paper inside hers. "Where's this coming from, sweetie? I think it might be time to tell you you're being silly now. What if you grow tired of me? What will you do?"

"I hadn't thought of that. I've just been worried that I might not be good enough for you, or that I might not live up to your standards."

Wes managed a rueful chuckle. "Sweetie, I don't have any standards for you to even try to live up to. This is new to me. We'll make our way. It sounds like you're worried about us getting married before we know each other well enough. I don't look at it that way. I hope it takes us the rest of our lives to get to know each other. I hope we're still discovering more about each other when we're in our eighties. How could you ever know whether you know someone well enough, anyway? There's no way to be sure."

"That's an interesting perspective. And it sounds romantic, too, continuing to learn about each other. I like that. It sounds like a way to keep things fresh. And… that brings me to the next item. What if I grow tired of living on a ranch? When I first found out Daddy wanted me to marry, my first thought was to marry someone other than a rancher."

Wes paused to consider what she'd said and think of his answer. "If that should happen, it could be a problem. But I don't think it will, and here's why. For one thing, you'll be a rancher's wife here and not a bored daughter left to her own devices. You and I will be partners in life, partners in the home and family, and partners in the business of ranching. I believe you'll be too absorbed in our life that you won't have time to grow tired of it. And I will make a commitment to you, here and now, that if you should find yourself growing bored or dissatisfied, I will move Heaven and Earth to find a solution. Will you make the commitment to me, to let me know if it begins to happen and not let it get so serious that it's a problem before I even know about it? Please don't keep that a secret from me. Matter of fact, please, let's don't have secrets from each other." He gave his head a shake. "Well, unless it's what I'm getting you for Christmas or something like that. Please, Nellie, let's take care of the little things before they become big ones. My strongest desire is for us to have a healthy, happy, loving, and joyous marriage."

"I'll make that commitment to you, Wes. I want those same things."

He leaned over and kissed the tip of her nose. "What else do you have on that paper? I'm feeling pretty good right now."

She grinned, then she looked back at her list and her smile faded. She took a deep breath. "You read Daddy's letter. You know how I've acted all my life, and you know what other people back home think of me." Nellie paused. "What will you do if my old habits and traits resurface and I do something that makes you angry?"

Wes looked down as he raised his eyebrows then looked back at her. He cocked his head. "Sweetie, I'm not sure silly is the right word, but I think you're borrowing future problems that may never happen."

"I know me, Wes. Far better than you know me. At some point, I don't know when, it's possible I might yell at you, argue with you, talk back, roll my eyes, stomp my feet, do all those things that earned me that spoiled reputation in the first place. I've tried to leave that attitude behind me and I've done well since Philip and Bethie arrived before Daddy died. I don't want to do that, I don't want to be like that or act like that. I promise you with all my heart I'll try to be a good wife and not let those old habits and attitudes come back. But we have to be honest and face it, a lifetime's habits are hard to break. They're ingrained in some ways and may come out before I even have a chance to think about it. I'm afraid of making you angry. I don't know how you act when you're angry."

"I can't remember the last time I was angry. I'm an easy-going man, and I'm pretty patient. It would take a lot on your part to make me angry."

"But if I do?"

"I think we already talked about things of this nature. Let's try to take care of situations before they get big enough for either of us to be angry. It's a two-way street, you know."

"But what if?"

He smirked. "Are you trying to make me angry now?"

"No, I'm not. And I would never do that just to see if I could."

"Good to know. All right. In his letter, your father said you needed a comeuppance and that you need structure and discipline. Now you haven't acted up since then that I know of, so I don't think a comeuppance is in order. And the structure and self-discipline that's required for keeping a home and ranch should provide what he thinks you've needed all along. Purpose and responsibility are good things, you know."

"Are you avoiding answering directly?" She looked at him skeptically.

"No, not on purpose. If you want a different answer, maybe you should ask the question differently. What exactly are you asking me?"

Nellie screwed up the courage to say the words she didn't want to say. "If I do something you think I shouldn't, will you... punish me?"

"You may be borrowing problems again, sweetie. You might be too busy doing all the right things to do something wrong."

"I hope that's the case. But I need an answer."

"How do you feel about that? It's usually a private matter with couples so I can't be sure, but I believe it's fairly common for that to happen, you know, a husband punishing a misbehaving wife. What are your thoughts?"

She started to give a serious answer then laughed. "It's not fair to ask me that. If I say I know it's commonly done, that's like giving you free rein to turn me over your knee."

He was silent. He was silent for so long, she called his name to get his attention.

He grinned with a devilish gleam in his eye. "I was imagining turning you over my knee."

"You want to cause me pain?"

"Hell, no. I want see your bare ass over my lap."

Nellie gasped with surprise. "Wes!"

"It was a mighty nice image. I'll hang on to that thought and enjoy it. Often."

"Are you saying you might spank me?"

"I think we should first try to avoid or prevent that, but if you're pressing me for an answer, then I'll have to say that it could happen if I see no other alternative. Does that answer the question?"

"Yes. I didn't think I'd get a *no* answer, but it's good to know you'll only do it if you don't see an alternative. I can live with that, I guess."

"Sure you can. And if it ever happens, I'm sure it'll be rare. Now, will you marry me?"

"Yes, I will."

He stood and punched his fist in the air a few times, then pulled Nellie to her feet, picked her up and twirled her around. When he set her down, he covered her face in little kisses as she laughed. It tickled.

"I hope you don't want a long engagement, sweetie. I want to marry you and get you moved in with me as soon as we can."

"I want to, too. We should do it before I get too settled in here with Philip and Bethie, just to have to turn around and move again. I want to get settled into my new home instead."

He kissed her again, one big, long kiss that didn't tickle.

❧

SUPPER WAS ENJOYABLE, especially since the boys had been fed early and were already tucked in bed. Philip and Wes enjoyed a bit of whiskey in celebration, while the ladies sipped a little of the men's but chose to drink iced tea for the most part. Wedding plans and moving were the main topics of conversation.

Philip proposed that they meet for lunch in town at Mary's restaurant, then afterward they could go talk to the pastor about scheduling the ceremony. Wes liked that idea and said they could pick out wedding rings and perhaps an engagement ring for her after they confirmed a time with Reverend Copperfield.

"What about a wedding dress, Nellie? Would you like to have one made? Mrs. Canfield does wonderful work. I don't think she does a lot of wedding gowns. Most of the ladies in town that I know of have just worn nice dresses instead of a white gown. What would you like to wear?"

Nellie didn't answer quickly.

"What would you like to do, sweetie? I'll buy you whatever you want."

"Oh, that's nice, Wes, but doesn't the bride's family usually take care of those things? I have plenty of money. If I get a dress, I think I'd like to buy my own. You know," she said with a glance at Philip, "I can finally act like a grownup."

"You could," Bethie said. "Or we could pay for it as a wedding gift. Like it or not, you're our family now."

Nellie's eyes glistened. "Well, now that you mention it, I was wondering, Philip, if you'd give me away. I think Daddy would like that. I know I would."

Philip put down his drink and his own eyes grew wetter. "Nellie, I would be most honored to stand in for your father. I'd be proud to walk you down that aisle."

Bethie did some comparatively quiet hollers and whoops right there at the table and the mood lightened. "I just had an idea," she said. "If Wes has time for us, we could load some of Nellie's things and after we get through doing things in town tomorrow, we could ride out and let Nellie see her new home. We can go ahead and start moving her things, at least the ones she won't need while she's here."

"Great idea," Wes agreed with a big goofy grin. "And you can see how badly this bachelor keeps house. But I don't even care, as long as we're making progress gettin' my gal moved in. I promise I'll hire someone to clean as soon as I can, and I hope it can happen before we marry."

"Speaking of which, let's get back to when we think that might be," Bethie said. "What's still up in the air that's keeping you from nailing down a date?"

"It could make a difference if I have a wedding gown made. I don't have to have one if it causes us to delay. I have nice clothes already."

Wes smiled at that, looking proud that she felt that way. Nellie thought that based on what he'd heard of her conduct in the past, he might have assumed she'd insist on the best of everything, down to the last detail. She felt proud, too. She didn't have to prove anything to anyone anymore, not even herself.

Philip chimed in. "You really don't have to be totally moved in, either. Your things are fine where they are until it's convenient to get them over there." He shrugged. "Tomorrow morning, you can select the things you'd like to have moved first, and we'll take them. We have to start somewhere."

"All right," Bethie said, "you don't have to wait for a dress, you'll get rings tomorrow, talk to the pastor tomorrow, nobody has anything they have to wait for. Why not get married Sunday, after the regular service? Most of the town will already be there anyway."

"This Sunday?" Nellie screeched.

"Sure," Wes said as he took her hand. "Let's do it, Nellie. It'll be perfect."

"This is so sudden! I expected more time."

"What do you need time for? You already said you wanted to

get settled into your new home as soon as possible. Sunday's probably as soon as possible," he said with a chuckle.

Nellie shrugged in resignation and exhaled deeply. "All right. Sunday it is."

Bethie clapped her hands together in a scheming sort of way. "Now. The rings. The mercantile keeps a modest assortment, but I want you to go to see Emmett Burke, the blacksmith."

"The blacksmith?"

"Yes. All right, he's a metal worker and works with all kinds of metals. He's an absolute artist, and he makes jewelry, too. He may have some already made up. If not, he can make what you describe to him or come up with an original design. Ask him to show you his own wedding band. It's extraordinary."

"That sounds interesting. I've never had jewelry made especially for me." She held out her hands. "I've never worn much jewelry at all. One of Mother's necklaces now and then, that's about it."

"Things are changing in a big way in your life, Nellie. So much is happening all at once, it seems like. How do you feel about that?" Philip asked.

"I miss Daddy, but I'm glad he's with Mother now. And I'm glad neither of them are hurting anymore. It took a lot of time to be able to remember my mother without wanting to cry, I think it's happening a little faster with Daddy's death. Maybe because I'm older."

"Maybe so," Philip said. "Are you ready to be an ol' married lady? Ready to be a rancher's wife?"

Nellie smiled and cut a sly look toward Wes. "As ready as I can be, I guess. I never helped out with the animals or any ranch business before, but Wes says he'll teach me. And he'll be patient."

Bethie laughed. "At least you've lived on a ranch. I was a city girl, born and bred. We never even had a cat. I swear, I had no clue about life on a ranch."

By the time she finished that last sentence, Philip was already starting to laugh. He loved this story; it never ceased to make him laugh.

"Go on," Bethie said, "I know you want to tell it."

Philip wiped his eyes. "She's telling the God's honest truth when she says she was clueless, at least about chickens and cows. Our girl here... was deathly afraid of the chickens."

"Well, they ran all around my ankles and pecked me! They ran me out of the pen." She looked directly at Nellie with big, round eyes. "They chased me right out of the pen. Evil chickens. Pure evil." Bethie shook her head and grinned at the memory.

"For weeks, I had to bring in the eggs every day before I could get her to go back out there. Then there was the cow. Oh, the cow." Philip started laughing again, the kind of laugh where he was crying big tears, nearly hysterical, and couldn't stop. "Now the big animals didn't scare her at all. Bethie was quite taken with cows."

"Those big, beautiful eyes," she said. "How can you not love those?"

"Anyway, at the time I had a small herd of Holsteins and I sold all but two of them right after we married. I wanted to keep those two to be our own dairy producers. Bethie named them Billie and Bessie."

"They were the sweetest things. I used to kiss and pet them like they were big dogs or horses. Bessie would see me in the mornings and greet me by nodding her head. She talked to me."

"She did. Bessie made sounds for Bethie that she didn't use with anyone else," Philip said. "Impressed me, for sure. Here was this city girl coming in and Bessie took to her right off. You'd swear they talked to Beth and she'd understand them. Bessie, and Billie for that matter, never gave Bethie a single problem when I was teaching her how to milk a cow. They were patient as could be. I have to admit, it was the darnedest thing."

"I just have a special way with cows. It's kind of a magical thing."

Philip started laughing again. "Well, maybe with our cows."

Bethie winked at Nellie. "Here we go."

Philip continued. "Bad storm came up one night, knocked a tree over and it hit a fence. Wasn't a big tree, but it was enough to take down one fence pole and bring down the fence on either side of it. Well, we got to checking around the next morning and Bessie was missing. She must have gotten out. A couple of men grabbed ropes and took off in opposite directions, north and south, to look for her. Bethie panicked over Bessie being out by herself and grabbed a rope, and she took off, too, headed west."

Philip appeared to be losing the fight to keep a straight face. "A little later I was helping the hands repair some damage to the barn. Before too long, one of the hands looked up and said, 'What the hell?' I looked up and couldn't believe it. Here came Bethie with a cow, all right, but it wasn't our cow. Bessie was a Holstein, white with big patchy black spots all over her. Bethie was pulling a Milking Shorthorn. She had a white face like Bessie's, but her spots were red and roan. She didn't look a thing like our cow."

Even Bethie was laughing.

"So I walked out and met them. 'Bethie, honey, did you have any problems getting Bessie home?'"

Wes' body shook with his laughter, but he tried not to be so loud as to interrupt or keep Philip from finishing the story. Nellie laughed, too, her hand over her mouth as though she couldn't believe it.

Philip continued as he wiped his eyes with his handkerchief again. "Bethie said, 'She didn't want to come with me at first, I had to sweet talk her a lot. I think she was probably still scared from the storm.' Bethie stroked the cow's face and nuzzled against it, and the poor beast was warming up to her.

"I said, 'Bethie, honey, this isn't our cow. Ours is black and white. This is one of Derek's Shorthorns. He must have had some damage over at his place, too.'"

"I've never been so embarrassed in my life, but when I stood back and took a good look at that poor confused cow, I could plainly tell it wasn't Bessie," Bethie explained. "That poor cow. I don't know where my head was. I was so worried about her and when I saw a cow out of place, I guess I just knew it had to be ours."

"What happened to Bessie? Did you get her back?" Nellie asked.

"Oh, sure. One of the other men found her. She was fine," Philip said. "We got Derek's cow back to him and we all lived happily ever after."

Wes jiggled Nellie's hand. "I hope you aren't still worried about not knowing how to take care of ranch animals."

She chuckled. "No, not after that story. I might not have done any better, but I'm pretty sure I wouldn't do any worse."

"There you go," Bethie said. "Just remember, Nell, it's all a big adventure. Things work out the way they should. They always do."

WES WAS ALREADY SEATED at the table when Nellie and the Hickams arrived and he wasn't alone. Harriet and Arthur Smithers were with him. Harriet spotted them coming in the door first and jumped up to greet Nellie.

"You have to be Nellie. I am so thrilled to meet you. Even though you didn't come to Operation Big Rock Brides in our normal manner, I sure am glad you came to us." Harriet gave Nellie a big, long hug before she put her hands on the young woman's shoulders, holding her at arm's length, and sized her up. "My, my, you are a pretty thing. It's no wonder Wes fell head over heels for you." She leaned in closer to Nellie. "I'll tell you something. Of the men I spoke to about you, Wes was the one I hoped would step up. I just had a good feeling about you two. When he read your father's letter, he didn't see a description of a spoiled or undesirable girl, the way the other men did. He saw a father's love and concern for the person who was dearest to him. I knew right then he would be the perfect match for you."

"Thank you," Nellie said. She wasn't exactly sure thanks were appropriate, then remembered Harriet said she was pretty. Thanks were definitely appropriate. Then she couldn't think of what else to say, so she smiled.

"Now when you two get settled in, Arthur and I would love to drop by and give you a special little gift. It's not much, just a little token, really, but it's something we decided to give to all of our mail order couples."

"How lovely, I look forward to it," Nellie said. She thought about inviting them for supper one evening, then decided she'd better talk to Wes first and see if he agreed. She thought it best not to overstep even before they were wed.

Arthur and Wes stood and the Smitherses said their good-byes. Wes reached out for Nellie's hand, pulled her to him and kissed her cheek. Mostly her cheek, a bit of lip was included. She looked around to see if anyone noticed.

He pulled out her chair again. Wes held her hand and Nellie liked that. She liked how it showed the world that he had claimed her. She liked that his hand felt so big and strong around hers, giving her a secure feeling. She liked that he occasionally moved a finger or two so it gently massaged her hand. She imagined it touching her body like that in other places. *Don't forget to talk to Bethie about sex.*

When their food arrived and they got settled down, Bethie asked Nellie if she had any specific song requests for her to sing at the wedding. She didn't, so Bethie made a few suggestions and they narrowed it down to one song to be sung just before the vows.

"This is almost embarrassing to admit, but I've never even been to a wedding," Nellie said. "I'm nervous about it."

"Oh, Nell, don't be," Bethie said. "We'll talk to the pastor and his wife and they'll put you at ease, I'm sure. Charlotte Copperfield will, especially. She directs the activity at our weddings and she's good at it. She'll tell you exactly what to do. Reverend Copperfield is good, too. I like that he keeps weddings short and doesn't try to insert a sermon like other preachers do sometimes."

"Besides," Philip added, "if he keeps people there a long time after the regular service and keeps all those men from getting their Sunday dinner, he'll have some fights on his hands. Trust me, he'll keep it short."

"All right," Nellie said. "I will feel better if she'll go over everything with me."

"We can even practice it if you like, go through the motions. Philip can walk you down the aisle, figure out exactly where to stand, that sort of thing."

"Perfect!" Nellie said.

After lunch, they all traveled the short distance to the church and the parsonage across the road from it. Nellie rode with Wes in his buggy. The Copperfields heard the horses and came outside to greet their company.

"Hello," Charlotte said. "I believe we know everyone except this young lady. You're Nellie Lancaster, aren't you?" she asked. At Nellie's startled look, she whispered with a grin, "I'm in the Ladies' Aid Society. I knew the Hickams would be bringing you home with them."

"Ahh," Nellie said in understanding.

"I'm Charlotte, the pastor's wife, and this is my husband, Reverend Copperfield. It's good to have you here, dear. Let's go on in the house and sit down and you can tell us what we can do for you."

Nellie felt welcomed and decided she liked Charlotte.

Once inside, Wes got around to telling them why they were there. "Reverend, Nellie has agreed to become my wife, and we want to get married as soon as we can. We were hoping you'd be willing to perform a simple, short ceremony for us this Sunday right after the church service. We figured it made sense to do that since nearly everyone in town will be there anyway."

"Well, first, let me congratulate you both," the pastor said. "And, of course, it would be my pleasure to perform the ceremony. After church Sunday will be perfect. I can mention it and invite everyone when I make other announcements at the start of the service."

"Bethie, are you going to sing?" Charlotte asked.

"Yes, I am," she answered. "I thought I'd stay at the piano bench at the close of service and play us right on into the wedding."

"Perfect," Charlotte said. "Nellie, will you need to change clothes before the ceremony, or will you already be wearing the dress you'll be married in?"

"I'll be wearing it. I decided not to get a special wedding gown."

"Wonderful! That'll simplify things."

"Yes, it will," the pastor agreed. "At the close, I'll tell people to remain in their seats but to feel free to talk and mingle. Nellie, you and Wes and Charlotte will get up from where you've been sitting and go to the back."

"Oh, Reverend, I'm sorry to interrupt, but Philip is going to walk me down the aisle."

"All right, then, you four will get up and go to the back. I'll give a signal and Bethie will sing. When the song is over, Charlotte will tell you to walk up front and stand beside me, Wes." Wes nodded. "When the time is right, we'll give a signal and Charlotte will let you two know it's time to walk down the aisle. Philip, when you get to the front, stand there while I ask who gives her away, then you can answer however you feel best. I'll read a scripture or two, remind you both this is a lifetime commitment, until one of you passes over. You'll repeat vows, exchange rings if you have them, and I'll join you in holy matrimony. After the kiss, I'll let you know to turn and face the congregation and I'll introduce you as Mr. and Mrs. Hollicker. I'll send you down the aisle to the door while Bethie plays a happy processional. Then the people will congratulate you as they exit. And that will be that. Any questions?"

"Yes," Nellie spoke up.

"What is it, Miss Nellie?"

"When we do the vows and I have to repeat them, will you keep it to short phrases? I know I'm going to be nervous and I don't want to forget or make a mistake."

He patted her shoulder. "I will keep them short, I promise. Although, I always think it's sort of charming when that happens."

THE NEXT STOP was the smithy, or the "Metal Works" as the sign said. Wes introduced his fiancée to Emmett and told them they wanted rings for their wedding on Sunday.

Emmett congratulated them and reached down behind the counter for a ring display tray and set it on the counter. "This is what I have now, but I can make new rings for you if you have any idea of what you'd like."

"Emmett, show them yours. They might get an idea of the kind of work you can do," Bethie suggested.

"Of course," he said as he pulled off his wedding band and handed it to Nellie. "I can do something similar if you like it, but I like to keep the sets one-of-a-kind, so it won't be identical to that one."

"This is beautiful," Nellie said, then she handed it to Wes to look at. She leaned over to look at the rings in the tray. She picked up one that caught her eye. It had the cursive letter B and designs around it. "I like this. What can you do with the letter H?"

Emmett reached under the countertop again and pulled out a pencil and a piece of paper. He drew something and then turned it to face the engaged couple. It was a leaning capital letter H with two interlaced hearts that made up the horizontal crossbar of the letter.

"Oh, Emmett, that would be incredibly intricate and tedious to make. You'd have to make those hearts so small!" Nellie said.

He laughed. "I wouldn't call it tedious. I'd call it exquisitely detailed. I could put some kind of simple designs around the rest of the band." He pulled out another tray. "Take a look at the belt buckles. Some of these designs might look nice on a ring. Smaller, of course."

"I think I prefer it without anything else added to it," she said and pointed to some rings in the tray. "Can you make it look like these rings? Where the raised design looks burnt or burnished at the base? That really sets off the design. I like the old, primitive feel it evokes."

"Sure. I can do that," Emmett said. "I like it, too. I'm going to call this design Hollicker Hearts."

"Emmett!" Wes exclaimed. "I believe you just named our ranch. The *Hollicker Hearts Ranch*. Nellie, I'm going to have a big sign made to go across the driveway. It'll have this design with the words Hollicker Hearts Ranch. It'll look beautiful."

"Do you want a wood sign or a metal sign?" Emmett asked.

Wes looked at him, his new excitement still clear on his face. "Oh, it would be a powerful sign in metal, wouldn't it?" he asked Emmett, who agreed.

"It will be if I make it," Emmett said with a grin.

"Nellie, it'll be our brand! Emmett, I need you to make me a branding iron with this design, too."

"I'd be happy to," he said. "I'll have the rings done Saturday, but it'll be a while before I have the sign and the iron ready."

"Perfect,"

"One last thing." Emmett handed them a string that had several rings attached, starting with a small one and each successive ring graduated in size. There was a number on each ring. "Try these on your ring fingers and tell me what size each of you need."

When they left, Nellie thought Wes might now be even more excited than she was.

Outside, Wes helped Nellie back into the buggy. As soon as she was seated, Bethie came running up to their side. "We need to make a quick stop, maybe ten or fifteen minutes. You two go on; we won't be far behind you."

"Are you sure? Is everything all right?" Nellie asked.

Bethie dismissed them with a wave of her hand. "Don't be silly. Everything's fine. I'm giving you fifteen minutes of alone time, now get on out of here."

Wes laughed and *hyahed* the horses into action.

"Do you think everything's all right?" she asked.

He laughed. "Don't know, don't care. As soon as we turn onto that road ahead and get out of sight, I'm going to stop this buggy and lay a lip lock on you that'll take your breath away."

"Ohh," she said. "Won't these ponies go any faster?"

"So you like kissing, do you?"

"So far, I'd have to say yes."

"Good thing. It's something I like to do, too."

"Can you believe we'll be married in three days?" Nellie asked him.

"I'm counting the hours. Before long, I'll probably start counting minutes, too."

"Really? I didn't know men got excited about weddings."

"I'm not excited about the wedding."

"Then what?"

"I'm excited about after the wedding and getting you back home, all to myself. And we won't have to stop at kissing anymore."

Nellie smiled but got quiet at the thought.

"Sweetie, are you nervous about our wedding night? Or wedding afternoon, as it were?"

"Not really nervous. I'm excited, too, even eager. It's odd because I don't know just exactly what I'm eager for. Sort of, but not specifically. Not exactly. But I know when you kiss me, I go all soft inside and then I feel different. I can feel a warmth, a heat start to build down there."

"Sweetie, we've only really kissed three or four times."

"I know. That's why I think when we, you know, do more than kissing, then—"

"Fuck. When we fuck, you mean," he said, cutting off her words.

"That's a swear word. I've heard the hands say it when they didn't know I was around."

"It's a swear word when it's used like that. Not in the bedroom, though. It's a most excellent word in the bedroom. I hope you'll say it. I will."

"All right, anyway, when we do more than kiss, I know it's bound to feel even that much better than just kissing, right?"

"Sweetie, you don't know how much I wish I could make these horses fly so I could get you home and show you right now what it feels like."

She sighed in mock exasperation. "Neither of these horses is named Pegasus, so I don't think that's going to happen."

He reached a spot that was hidden from view from the main street. Wes wasted no time pulling Nellie into his arms and kissing her. Between fevered assaults on her mouth, he whispered how much he wanted to touch her and kiss her all over, to deliver sweet torment, and finally fuck her. He stopped the kiss and pulled her away from him just enough to have room to cup her breasts. "I can't wait to kiss these and suck on them," he said as he squeezed and moaned in pleasure.

"Oh, Wes, that feeling I get, it's building up. Down there."

"I hope so, sweetie, that's good. You should be getting nice and wet down there. That's how your body gets ready to accept mine. To accept this," he said as he put her hand on his hardness. "I can hardly wait until you can touch it without these clothes between us. I can hardly wait to feel it inside you, make you mine. Oh, sweet Nellie."

He backed away. "We'd better stop. They'll catch up with us soon. I need time to cool down some and let this thing shrink down to its normal state."

"Well, you were right about one thing. You took my breath away."

Wes chuckled, low and sexy. He gave her one last sideways hug and kissed her on the temple, then took up the reins again. Soon they were in motion, each lost in thoughts and anticipation of Sunday afternoon.

They came to a particularly bumpy spot in the road and Wes slowed the horses so they wouldn't chance throwing a wheel. "Jake and I try to keep the worst holes filled along this road. We'll do that to these holes when they get a little worse."

"What do you fill them with?"

"Rocks and dirt. Believe it or not, we found it's best to do it during a light rain. The dirt packs down better and the wind doesn't blow it away."

"Hmm. Do you have to do it a lot?"

"No, not really. Besides, we don't get a lot of rain around here. So, sometimes we just have holes in the road."

She chuckled. "I suppose worse things could happen."

"That's how we see it. We're about the only ones who ride this road anyway."

"That must make it nice and private on the ranch."

"It does. We like it that way. Our ranch is next to Ruby's, but you can't see the houses from each other's place. We pass their place, then ours is a little bit down the road and around the next bend. It's close, but seems farther away. Does that make sense?"

"It does. I think I'll like being alone with you, far away from anyone else."

"Yes, ma'am. I've been hoping you would. Three more days and you'll see what it's like."

"I want to get married, I do, but everything's happening so fast, it almost doesn't seem real. Is there any possibility we're jumping the gun?"

"If we waited, what would we be waiting for?"

She thought about the question and giggled. "I don't have an answer for that. For love? I think we're on our way to that. For propriety? I don't think either of us cares much about that. Besides, this is a mail order bride town and people are accustomed to near-strangers marrying. All right, maybe it's not too soon after all. You seem to have a reasonable argument for everything."

He laughed and winked at her. "It's all those debate classes at the university. I was very good at it."

"Well, you might have told me that at the outset. I might not have agreed to marry you if I knew I faced a lifetime of losing arguments."

"Then I'd say I'm also wise for not mentioning it."

"You'll have to teach me some strategies."

He burst out laughing. "Not on your life. I'd like to continue winning our debates."

"Maybe we won't have too many, at least not until I've learned a few tricks of my own."

"Won't help. I'll always win."

Surprised, she looked at him and saw his grin. "Just a little bit on the cocky side, aren't you?"

"No, no, no, not cocky. Truthful. That's what it is, truthful."

Nellie cocked an eyebrow toward him and grinned, then was silent for a while. "Wes, have you ever been in love before?"

"No, I haven't. There was a young lady I was interested in during my college years, but nothing came of it."

"Were you, um, intimate with her?"

"No, just a few kisses. As pleasant as they were, neither of us felt the relationship going further than that."

"Have you known, I mean, have you had..." She couldn't finish the question.

"Are you asking how many women I've known intimately?"

"Yes." She looked down, unable to look him in the eye.

"I don't know for sure."

She looked up, an odd look on her face. "That many? You said you'd never been in love, so I thought maybe there weren't... many."

"Ah, I see. You know, you don't have to be in love to want a sexual release. It was mostly in college. Understand, brothels do well in college towns. And word gets around among the men if there are places to meet, well, loose women. So there were opportunities. And if there's one thing true of every college man I ever met, they take advantage of such opportunities. We're like animals. Dogs. Rabbits, all of us."

Nellie was grinning by that point. "I think I can live with that answer. So I don't have to wonder about the woman who got away?"

"No, ma'am, you surely don't."

"I almost wish you had reason to be jealous of my past, but you know it already. No man in a fifty mile perimeter of Newport had any interest in me." Her voice sounded wistful, almost sad.

"That's only because they didn't know you the way I do. If any had truly taken the time to get to know you deep down, we'd be having an entirely different conversation."

She smiled at him and put her hand tentatively on his knee. "Thank you for saying that."

He took her hand in his. "You're welcome, sweetie. It's the truth, you know."

As they neared Jake and Ruby's place, he started telling her about it. "They have a nice big house that Jake's father built, anticipating a large family, but that didn't happen. He used to have two barns, but one burned down. It's a nice working ranch. When we built my place, both the house and the barns, he told me the things he'd do differently and the things he wanted on his ranch but didn't have yet. I included some of those ideas in mine from the start instead of waiting to add later."

"That sounds smart, listening to the voice of experience. I was never good at that, I'm told."

"You need to stop thinking that way about your past, that it's a string of failures or disappointments. Don't you realize that everything you've done in your life, every choice you've made and all the things that happened to you are what made you the woman you are now? I don't know if you've noticed, but I happen to be extremely fond of that woman."

"I'll have to think about that philosophy."

"Do that. Up ahead's their ranch; you can see it now. If they're outside, we might stop and say hello." He laughed. "Or maybe just slow down and say hello. I want to get you home so you can see your house."

"I'll be sure to wave frantically as we pass. I want to see my home, too."

No one was outside at the Jernigan place, so they sailed on down the road. When they went around the bend in the road and Nellie caught sight of the ranch house, her eyes widened and her chin dropped.

"Wes, it's beautiful! And so big. I'm surprised at how big it is. I thought our house back home was big, and it was bigger than most, but this is amazing."

"Now you know why I want someone to share it with. A big house is lonely for one person. And now you can also understand why I have to neglect parts of it."

"I see why."

"Stop worrying, I can already see what you're thinking. I'll get you plenty of help with chores. I don't want you overwhelmed."

"Seeing this house, I appreciate that more than I ever thought I would."

Wes drew the buggy to a stop, away from the porch steps so Philip could bring the wagon up close. He jumped down and helped Nellie to the ground.

"Should I carry you over the threshold now, or wait until Sunday?"

"I think wait until Sunday for that. Wes, I love this porch. I don't think I've ever seen one so big."

"I wanted it to be extra wide and protected enough to still be able to sit out here in the rain. I've always loved rainstorms."

"So do I," she said with an appreciation for something else they had in common.

He gave her a brief tour, then they went back into the parlor. She told him what was on the wagon and they moved some things to make way for the new items. He had already made space for her things in the closet and dresser.

When they moved the things out of the way and there was really nothing else to do, Nellie came up behind Wes and tapped him on the shoulder. "How about a few more of those kisses until they get here?"

"I'm not sure that's a good idea. You know what kissing you does to me. That's not something Philip and Bethie need to see first thing when they walk in."

She shrugged. "All right, I'll let you get by with that this time, but in my mind, oh, we are kissing."

"Damn, woman. That alone was enough to get me started," he said as he adjusted himself. "Maybe we need to talk about something that won't get me excited. We could talk about the ranch budget. Recite your favorite recipes. How about that?"

Just then they heard the clip-clop of the horses. "Whew," Wes said, and Nellie laughed at him.

It took a good bit of time for the men to wrangle the bigger crates off the wagon. Instead of trying to get the larger ones inside, they opened them on the ground and carried the packed items in separately. The loveseat was the biggest thing on this trip, and the men good-naturedly questioned her choice of bringing it. In the end they all agreed it looked perfect in the parlor among his original furniture.

"I can only offer you whiskey, water, or milk. What would everyone like?"

Nellie helped him prepare the drinks, and she was immensely pleased to see an icebox in his kitchen, too. "This is very modern. It's going to be nice working in this kitchen."

"I wanted to go ahead and put in as much as I could. We have a flush toilet and running cold water. I considered including running hot water, but that'll have to be done later. It was the only thing I purposely chose to postpone until later."

"I might not know what to do with myself if I had hot water on tap. I'd feel like a queen or something."

"Well, someday you shall have it."

They had a nice visit with the Hickams until Philip and Bethie decided it was time to go. "We still have to go to Molly's and pick up the boys."

Wes thanked them again for the moving help. Philip stood and took his and Bethie's glasses to the kitchen. "We'll be in the wagon," he said as he pulled Bethie along. "And come for supper again tomorrow night." It was clear he was giving Wes and Nellie a little privacy to kiss goodnight.

~

THE NEXT MORNING when things quieted after breakfast and cleanup, Nellie asked Bethie if she had time for a chat.

"Of course, I do. Will we want tea?"

"We might."

Bethie put on water to boil then sat down at the table with Nellie.

"Mother died before marriage was even on my horizon and I could never talk to Daddy about these things. Mrs. Nelson wouldn't talk to me about them. Will you tell me what I need to know about, you know, the intimacies of marriage? The physical side?"

Bethie grinned as though she'd been given a long-awaited gift. "I would love to talk about it. I wondered if you would ask me. I was prepared to mention it tomorrow if you hadn't said anything yet."

"Oh, good. I'm so glad to have a woman I can trust to talk to."

"My mother wouldn't talk about it. All I could get from her was that my husband would teach me what he wanted me to know. And that's exactly what happened, but not the way Mother probably envisioned. Besides, they never expected me to marry anyway."

"You have me curious now. Tell me!"

"I was such an innocent." She laughed. "And I fell head over heels for Philip when we first met. It was mutual. We were both staying with Derek and Molly at the time. One day Philip wanted to take me to town and spend the day with me. I was so excited. We stopped along the way at an old, abandoned house and he proposed. It was this very property. He knew he wanted to buy it and build our home here. Anyway, of course, I said yes. I wanted to make sure he knew just how innocent I was in case he was expecting a woman who knew what she was doing, because I knew absolutely nothing. I kept asking him questions and he kept answering them, all the rest of the way into town. My questions now seem so silly but we both treasure our memories of that day. We both knew by the time we got to town, we would never have a problem talking to each other about sensitive things. And sure enough, we haven't."

"That sounds so sweet. I hope to be that open with Wes."

"There's no reason why you can't be. If you want to talk about something embarrassing or touchy, just say it. Don't give him a chance to think it's improper. He'll appreciate that you have that level of trust with him."

"I hadn't thought about that. I was just thinking of what it would be like from my point of view, how potentially embarrassed I'd be."

"Well, fortunately, I had no such compunction. We talked about which is the right hole, how an erection forms and how it spurts out his seed, how I might bleed a little bit the first time, all those things. It's a wonder he didn't laugh me right off that buggy, but he didn't."

"Yes! Those are the kind of things I need assurance about. Let's talk about that bleeding thing first."

"All right. I bled a little bit, but not much at all. I understand some women don't. We had a towel under me, just in case. I was worried about blood stains on the sheets."

"I'll have to remember that."

"Do you have any specific questions?"

"No, not really specific questions, just vague worries. I mean, how do you know what to do? What if I do something he doesn't like?"

"Oh, Nellie, hon, I think that's part of the beauty of the act. You don't have to know what to do. You feel. You feel what he's doing, you feel your own emotions, and everything just seems to work together. You'll find yourself wanting to explore his body, to touch him and see how he responds to your touch. Do it; don't hold back or wait for him. You'll want to cover him in kisses in a way and in places you can't imagine right now. It's a passion you want to speed up and slow down at the same time.

As far as being afraid you'll do something he doesn't like, well, unless you leave the bed, or wherever you are at the time, then there's no such thing as something he doesn't like."

Nellie giggled a little at that. "The way you describe it, it sounds beautiful, almost mystical or magical."

"It can seem that way. I've felt such a deep connection with Philip at those times, it's hard to explain. I feel so close to him, and I feel complete. But then there are those times when it's not very mystical, especially after babies come along. Instead of spending afternoons in bed like you used to, you'll only have about five minutes to accomplish the deed. But it's still good."

"Really? It's still worth it for so short a time?"

Bethie poured the hot water into the teapot and brought it to the table.

"Most definitely. Sex can be different each time. I think it should be. It might get stale if you did the same thing every time, in the same manner, like you're checking things off a list. What makes it different each time are the emotions you bring to it. Relations can be sweet, sentimental, hot, passionate, frenzied, angry, dirty, punishing, easy, whatever your moods at the time."

"Really? Angry? You have sex when you're angry? Seems like that would be the last thing you'd want to do."

Bethie leaned over for emphasis. "It's some of the best. A lot of people, especially women, probably think that way. But oh, are they missing out. Talk about frenzied. That angry passion makes the physical side, well, angrier." She chuckled at her inability to describe it. "Forget the soft touches and sweet caresses. This whole other element comes in, and the heat level rises to furnace hot. It's rough, nothing gentle going on. And it's one of the most exciting things you'll ever experience."

"And that makes the anger go away?"

"No, it's not magic. But it does change the dynamics. It's like deep down you both realize it's not the two of you fighting each other. It's the two of you together fighting whatever the problem is. I find it makes it easier to resolve the problem after that, since it relieves all that tension and pent-up emotion. No more finger-pointing and placing blame. My only regret is that Philip and I rarely get angry any more. We get along so well together, we don't ever fight."

"If you truly can talk to him about anything, you should tell him you want to have angry sex without actually being angry."

Bethie picked up the teapot and began pouring. "That's exactly what I do."

"I'm so glad I have you to talk to," Nellie said. "It has been so long since I have had anyone to talk to like this."

"I know women who did have someone to talk to—their own mothers—and their mothers gave them awful advice. I know one woman whose mother told her sex is dirty and something the woman has to endure for her husband's sake so she can give him children. I can't help but believe that the mother was just too embarrassed to talk about it. Surely, she couldn't actually believe that. What a miserable existence that would be if she did."

"I don't imagine the father in that case was exceptionally happy, either," Nellie said with a wry grin and a raised eyebrow. Bethie laughed out loud.

"Or maybe he wasn't too impressive with his efforts," Nellie added and they both laughed out loud.

"I wonder what that mother's mother told her," Bethie said. "Could have been a family tradition to loathe sex."

"What a sad thought, and I haven't even had sex yet."

"Nellie, be bold with it. Be adventurous. Participate. Actively participate, with emphasis on the being active part. Let yourself enjoy it. Lose yourself in it. You'll never regret it, and it'll keep getting better."

"Well, I'm excited about it now instead of apprehensive. Thank you."

"Oh! Wait. We never got you any honeymoon type night-gowns. Come with me. I'll give you some of mine."

"Oh, I couldn't take anything like that," Nellie said.

"Why not?" Bethie asked.

"Well, all right, I can't think of a good reason, but it doesn't seem right."

"Hogwash. I have so many, I'll never even notice they're gone." She went to her dresser and opened the second drawer. "Yes, I think this one. And this one. Oh, and the lavender one, too."

"That's too many!"

"Hogwash again. Here, look at these."

"Why, they look brand new. Have you ever even worn them?"

"A few times. The thing is, they never seem to stay on for very long before they land on the floor or get slung over a chair. You won't be wearing them for a long time, I promise."

"Hmm. I bet Wes will love these."

"I guarantee he will."

When Wes arrived early for supper, Bethie again sent them out to the gazebo with glasses of iced tea so they could talk more privately.

"I sure do like Bethie," Wes said. "She knows I want to be alone with you."

"I like her, too. She's become dear to me. I had a long talk with her this morning and now I feel I'm more ready for the intimate part of marriage."

"Sweetie, I didn't know you were concerned about that. You should have told me so."

Nellie laughed. "That's one of the things Bethie said. She said you and I should be able to talk about anything. Anything, no matter how embarrassed I may be to bring it up."

"Good for her. I agree. I don't want you to ever be embarrassed to tell me anything or ask me anything. What else did she say?"

"We talked about the physical side. Sex. I need to get where I can talk about it with you comfortably." She straightened and took a deep breath. "Sex. We talked about sex."

"Good for her again. What did you discuss about it?"

"That I shouldn't be worried about my first time."

"Were you? I didn't realize that, either, sweetie."

"Well, I'm not anymore. Matter of fact, I'm looking forward to it. As much as you are."

Wes laughed. "I doubt that, but it's nice to hear you're eager for it."

"I was afraid I'd do something wrong or do something you didn't like."

Wes didn't stifle his grin very well. "What did she say about that?"

"The same thing you're thinking right now. That when it comes to sex, there's probably nothing a man won't like."

"Oh, good for her again."

"It reminded me of what you said about college men."

"It doesn't stop when we graduate. We're like that until we can't do it anymore."

"The main thing she advised me was to just let go and have fun. It's no time to be inhibited."

"I need to send that woman flowers."

"No. You need to kiss me."

"Oh, I do?"

"Yes. She said I should let you know what I want when it comes to these things."

"You should definitely let me know."

They kissed, sweetly and slowly.

"I like doing this," she whispered.

"I do, too," he whispered back. "Let's make sure we do it a lot."

# CHAPTER 6

Sunday morning, they rose early, and Nellie spent extra time on her bath. She used her favorite bath oil and bath powder and even dabbed a bit of perfume on her wrists. Bethie helped her with her hair. The last thing she did was put all her remaining toiletries and clothing in a bag to take since she wouldn't be coming back to the Hickam ranch. She'd be going to her own. It excited her to think about that, and she wished the church service and the wedding were already over and she was headed home with her new husband.

They skipped Sunday School but were early for church, so they waited outside around some picnic tables until the classes were dismissed. Wes arrived shortly after they did, and Nellie walked over to greet him.

"Is that a new suit?" she asked. "You look extra handsome."

"It is new. I'm glad you like it. You look beautiful in that dress." He leaned over so only she would hear and whispered, "I can't wait to take it off you."

"Me, either," she managed to say before Philip and Bethie joined them.

"It's time for dismissal; let's go on in and claim our seats," Philip said.

Charlotte Copperfield found them and went over the plans again. The pastor stopped by briefly and made sure they all understood the plans, too. He told them again how happy he and his wife were for them.

Nellie wondered all through the service if Wes was able to get anything out of the sermon. She certainly wasn't. She kept thinking about the things Bethie said and wondered just how her afternoon would unfold. Occasionally, she felt a pang of guilt for thinking of such things in church, but she couldn't help it. She hoped God would understand, and rationalized that He ordained the covenant of marriage and the relations therein. Surely, He wouldn't mind if she thought about it on the day of her wedding.

It wasn't long before the sermon was over and church was dismissed. Time had passed so slowly for the last hour, and now it flew by so fast, she would hardly remember it later. Bethie's song was beautiful, but Nellie knew it would be. She didn't remember which verses the minister mentioned in his comments, but she did remember that she didn't mess up when she repeated her vows. She was so glad. She also remembered the sweet kiss when Reverend Copperfield said, "You may now kiss the bride." And she remembered how she was nearly overcome with joy and pride when he introduced them as Mr. and Mrs. Wes Hollicker.

It took less time than Nellie expected to get through all the people in line at the door to congratulate them. Bethie and Philip were last in line, on purpose.

"We have a wedding gift for you. I wanted you to always remember this day, so we asked Caleb Carter, you know, he's the newspaper editor, to bring his camera today. He's going to take a couple of photographs of you two on the front steps of the church."

Nellie threw her arms around Bethie. "I can never thank you enough for all you and Philip have done for me."

"Now don't start crying; you're about to have your photograph taken."

Bethie shooed everyone away from the church entrance so they could get on with it. She made sure Nellie's hair was in place, her dress was straight, and her cheeks were pinched pink.

When Caleb was finished, Bethie made sure the last of Nellie's things were in Wes' buggy. "Now, you two get on out of here. You've got a honeymoon to get started, and time's a-wastin'."

Nellie thanked them both again and Wes helped her into the buggy. He jumped in, gave her a kiss, and they left amid shouts of congratulations and good luck from the people still gathered.

FOR SOME REASON, both of them instinctively felt the need to get out of sight of the people at the church quickly so they'd have more of a sense of privacy. There wasn't any conversation between them until they'd traveled a few blocks and made a couple of turns. There wasn't any verbal communication, but the looks and winks and furtive touches said volumes.

Once they felt freer, Wes took her hand. "Where would you like to go on our honeymoon, sweetie?"

"Oh, Wes, I don't want to go anywhere. So much has changed in my life, I just want to settle down to life with you. Besides, I just traveled by train and coach from Newport and I don't want to do that again anytime soon."

"I understand, but I really hate not being able to give you a honeymoon."

"How about if we postpone a trip for a few months, maybe a year? That's it, we could take a trip when we've been married a year and we can celebrate not only our wedding, but our anniversary, too."

"We can do that. Now you have a whole year to decide where you want to go. Anywhere in the whole wide world."

"Who'll take care of the ranch?"

"If my expansion plans go well, we'll have ranch hands by then. Jake and Ruby can check on things, too."

"Anywhere in the world?"

"Yes, ma'am. Anything your heart desires."

"I don't think I'll want to be away long enough to go overseas or anything. But I'll come up with something we both like, I promise. Besides," she said, cutting her eyes at him flirtatiously, "we might have a child by then. We might have to postpone the trip until our second anniversary."

"When was your last monthly?"

"Last week. Why?"

"You're more fertile midway between."

"It's embarrassing that you know more about this than I do."

"Don't be embarrassed; you simply had no one to turn to for that kind of information. When you're a horny college man, you find out everything you can about these things. That's not a good time for fatherhood."

"Horny?"

"In an amorous mood, shall we say."

"Then it's fair to say I'm horny right now."

"Dear Lord, horses, learn to fly!"

When they reached the ranch house, Wes ran around to Nellie's side and picked her up, not even putting her on the ground.

"I'm going to carry my blushing bride over the threshold, my dearie. Then I plan to have my way with you," he said as he raised his eyebrows twice in a villainous expression.

Wes managed to turn the doorknob and he kicked the door wide open with his foot. He kissed her before he set her on her own feet, then he kissed her again, cupping her buttocks and breasts with increasing intensity.

"Aren't you hungry? It's past lunchtime," Nellie said.

Wes chuckled. "I'm starving, but I'll just have to suffer. Sustenance will have to wait until I've truly made you mine. I fried extra bacon this morning so we could have a quick, easy meal later. You don't know how I've wanted this, wanted you."

"I think I do, hon," she said, running her hand down the buttons on his shirt. "Will you give me a few minutes to get ready for you? Bring in my bag that's still on the buggy? Maybe you could go ahead and tend to the horses so you won't have to stop for that later."

He sighed in mock frustration then grinned at her. "Get ready for me?"

"I hope you like it."

"Nice. A sweet mystery to think about while I put the horses up." He gave her forehead a quick kiss. "I'll go get your bag."

SHE FRESHENED UP, let down her hair, put on the sheer nightie and waited for him. She wasn't sure if she should wait in the bedroom or in the front parlor where he could see her when he first walked in. She chose the parlor. Should she be seated? Reclined on the couch? Standing? She chose to stand, then she paced. *Maybe he's giving me extra time to get ready.*

Wes rushed in, throwing the door open quickly. When he saw her, his face went slack and he exhaled slowly, ending with a slow shake of his head. His eyes twinkled and he grinned. "Nellie, sweetie, I definitely do like that. I like that a lot. Stand there and let me look at you. With that light from the window behind you, I can see your body's outline through the gown. You're a right vision, Nellie. You look perfect."

Nellie expected him to move but he didn't; he just stood

there staring as though he wanted to imprint the sight of her in his brain. She felt gratified, amused, and empowered at the same time.

"Husband, I think you have too many clothes on."

"Oh, you are right about that," he said as he rushed and fumbled taking off his jacket, bolo tie, and shoes and socks.

"I think you need some help," she said as she went to him and unbuttoned his shirt. He stopped undressing himself and let her do it.

"It does seem better when you do it."

She pulled the shirt out of his britches and slid it off his shoulders, then threw it over the back of the nearest chair. Nellie slowly stepped around him, touching his chest, back, and the muscles of his arm before stopping in front of him. She continued to caress his chest, teasing his nipples and running her fingers through the hair that grew down his torso. "I think you're beautiful, too," she said. "So strong and powerful." She stroked his arms again. "These make me feel so safe and secure when they're wrapped around me. Almost like you're giving me your strength."

Wes could take it no longer. He pulled her close and took her mouth in an urgent kiss.

Nellie felt his hardness growing against her and her own desire surged. She felt his hands all over her and ran her own hands over his chest again, then reached around to his back as far as she could reach and squeezed him closer for a moment.

When she put her hand on his length, Wes stopped kissing and watched her. He wanted to watch her exploration of him. She unbuckled his belt and began to unbutton his britches. When the buttons were undone, he swooped her up in his arms and carried her to the bedroom. He wasn't gentle when he placed her on the bed, and she understood the need. She felt it, too. He removed his remaining clothes and climbed into the bed with her, next to her.

Nellie took his hardness in her hand again and ran her hands over it, feeling the velvety soft mushroom head and marveling at the rigidity of the shaft. She ran her fingers over a jutting vein and traced down to the base. She took his sac in one hand and gently felt for what was inside, then went back to having both hands on his hardness. She heard Wes moan and she looked up at him. "Is it all right if I kiss it?"

He moaned again. "Yes, baby, if you want to. I would like that."

Nellie bent down and lathered soft, wet kisses up and down the length. Wes pulled her hair aside and held it back; she knew he must want to watch her. She felt his hand touch the side of her face. As she explored, she took the head in her mouth and teased the ridge around the top with her tongue.

"*Sweet Jesus.* Woman, I'm about to explode. I've never felt anything so good."

Nellie pulled her mouth away long enough to say, "Go ahead and explode. I'd like to see that."

He pushed her off him. "No. No, ma'am, not this time," he said as he pulled her gown over her head, pushed her down on her back, nudged her legs apart, and loomed over her. "I'll make you mine first."

WHEN THEIR PASSIONATE hunger was sated, they decided it was time to feed their physical hunger. As Nellie reached for her robe, Wes started toward the door.

"Aren't you going to put some pants on?"

"No, why?

"You're going in there naked?"

"Nobody's here but us, sweetie. I'll just have to take them off again when we finish lunch."

"I've never eaten naked. I've never been out of my own room naked."

"Then it's high time you did."

"But," she said, then she remembered Bethie's comment about actively participating and being adventurous. She shrugged and tossed the robe. "All right."

"Would you rather have bacon and scrambled eggs or a bacon and cheese sandwich? I fry the bread in butter."

"That sandwich sounds good."

"Or I could add scrambled eggs to the sandwich, too, if you want."

"No, too much trouble. It would take just that much longer to get you back in bed," she said, and he laughed.

"I wouldn't want to delay that. We'll skip the eggs. You just sit here and look pretty for me while I fix lunch."

"I'll be getting us something to drink."

"I'll do it. Sit. Rest. You want to be fresh for the next round, don't you?"

She grinned at him. "Yes, but I want you to be fresh, too, so I'll help."

"Wife, just a few hours ago you vowed to obey me." He put his hands on his hips. "Don't tell me you're breaking your vows already."

"All right, all right," she said, holding up her hands. "I surrender."

"Smart woman. You don't want to break those vows."

"Honor and obey, got it. I always wondered why women have to obey. Are men automatically right about everything? They can't be, you know. It would be against the odds for that to be true."

"Odds don't matter, sweetie. Shall I quote the obey passages from the Good Book? You heard the pastor during the wedding. It was quite clear."

"I didn't hear much of anything this morning, worship

service or wedding. My mind kept drifting to thoughts of this afternoon. Just so you know, it was even better than I imagined. A lot more fun."

"Well, I'm glad I came through for you. I did my best. I was a little worried because you had me so damn hot, it was over way too soon. Both times. It'll get better, I promise."

"Better? Better than that? I don't see how."

"Yes, better. I'll last longer. We'll try new things. As wonderful as it was, it'll get even better."

"We'd best eat fast, then. I can't wait to see what better is like."

THAT EVENING, Wes reluctantly pulled himself out of bed and pulled on his britches without putting his underpants on first. "I need to go make the rounds, make sure the animals are all right."

"I want to go with you! Give me a minute to get dressed."

"No need to. You will want shoes, though," he said with a grin.

"Wes, I couldn't go out like that!"

"Why, are you afraid the cows and horses are going to see your lady parts? I doubt if they'll care."

"Smart aleck," she chided. "What if Jake and Ruby drop in?"

"They won't."

"You can't be sure."

"Yes, I can. Jake knows I wouldn't take to him interrupting my wedding day. They won't show up. They'll wait until we show up at their place. There are just some things a man doesn't do to another one. But, really, you don't need to get all dressed up again."

"All right, I'll just put the gown and robe on."

"No! I'd hate for that gown to catch on something and rip. Just the robe. That's all you need. It covers everything, you know."

She shook her head, amused. "All right. Robe and shoes."

Nellie had only seen the barns from a distance and she was impressed when she got closer. "Why do you have two barns? Daddy only had one."

Wes laughed. "I guess because Philip has two. I don't have a good answer for that, except that I just wanted them. I told you Jake had two until someone burned one down. He was lucky his dad built the second one years ago."

"And you use both of them?"

"I do. It's good to separate calving mothers. Separate any you think might be sick. Good to have extra room for buggies and tools and such. They definitely get used. One day I might even have a third one."

"Really? Three barns?"

"I have plans to increase the size of the ranch. Not the acreage, but the amount of livestock. I own all the property on that side of the road, too, not just this side. I plan to fence all that in, put in another good-sized barn, and maybe concentrate that whole side for a dairy business."

"So, this is mainly a meat business now?"

"Mainly. The property boundaries are still staked out. One day soon, we'll take some time and ride the perimeter of our land."

"I'd love to do that. I have so much to learn. I never wanted to when I was at home, but I sure do now."

"Good. I'll teach you everything you need to know, as I learn it. I still don't know everything," he said. "The main thing I've learned is to listen to Jake and Philip. One day I hope to know as much as they do."

"You will, Wes. They've been doing this their whole lives. You've only been at it a year or two. This is amazing for that short a time. I'm proud of you."

He beamed. "I am pretty pleased with how it's going. All according to plan."

"You need to tell me about the plan. You have the room for more livestock. Looks like you could just go ahead and buy it. You can afford it."

"I could, but that's not a good way to increase a business. That's how people get into trouble, get more than they can handle. Besides, it's not financially responsible. Since it's a business, it needs to support itself once it gets started. I've already accounted for start-up costs, and now the business needs to make money. As it does, I'll put that money back into it. If we pour our personal wealth into it, it won't be controlled growth. As a matter of fact, that isn't a sustainable business plan and eventually the business will fail and we'll be broke."

"Oh. I don't want that. I never looked at it that way. I should have been listening to Daddy all these years."

He grinned at her. "Then you wouldn't be the same Nellie I fell for."

"Still, it seems like you could spend a little personal money once in a while."

"No, ma'am. Not going to do that, not while the business is successful. We're doing well now. I'm paying myself a decent amount and putting the rest into the ranch. I refuse to use our money unwisely. What if the cattle market busted for some reason and the business failed because of it? We'll need our personal wealth then. So the smart thing to do is protect it now. I won't spend our money on the ranch unless there's an urgent need."

"You have plenty of money, though. Or maybe I could invest some of mine in our business."

"No!" He whirled around to look squarely at her. "No, absolutely not. Your father gave that money to you, not to me. I won't take it. Besides, I want you to keep that money where it is, in the bank, earning interest. What if something should happen to me? If I die? I want you to have your own money to live on. That's your security for the future. That money stays there. Understand?"

"It's my money, Wes."

"And it'll stay your money, in the bank, working for you earning interest. No argument."

"But—"

"No, Nellie. We won't be buying livestock with your money. Period. I want you to leave your money where it is. I have plenty. We have a growth plan for the ranch and we'll stick to it. There's no reason to rush it."

"All right. I understand."

# CHAPTER 7

*W*es and Nellie did what newlyweds do for two or three more days, then they decided they'd go into town and pick up a few things at the mercantile. Wes wanted to talk to Shirley or Clint Keller to see if they knew of any women who might be interested in working two or three days a week to help with household chores and cooking. The Kellers owned the general store and not only knew everyone in town, but they knew everything that was going on in town. There was a good chance they'd know someone.

When they came to Ruby and Jake's house, Jake was outside. "How are the newlyweds this morning?" he asked as he stuck out his hand to shake Wes'.

"We're doing well, thank you. I thought I'd treat this lovely lady to a day in town, shop a little bit and go out to eat. Want us to pick up anything for you at the store?"

"No, I don't think we need anything that can't wait, but you can pick up our mail if we have any."

"We'll do that. Not sure exactly when we'll be back, but we'll stop by."

"I'll tell Ruby. See you later." He rapped the side wall of the wagon a couple of times as a goodbye.

Once on the road, Nellie said she hoped Ruby invited them in. She'd like to see inside their house.

"It's a nice one. You can tell it's a big house. Jake's parents wanted a large family, but they weren't so blessed. Did Bethie tell you the story of how Ruby came to Big Rock?"

"She didn't go into much detail. Just that Ruby led an unfortunate life and got into trouble with the law after her father died. I believe she said the judge took pity on her. She could have gone to prison, but instead, he sent her here to get married."

"That's it in a nutshell. Get Ruby to tell you sometime. The point I was getting at was that she went from having to steal and sneak into barns to sleep at night to having this huge ranch. It was hard for her, going from one extreme to another. I don't think she felt worthy at first. But she came out on this side all the better for it. She's one of the happiest people I know now."

"I look forward to getting to know her. Maybe she'll be like the sister I always wanted."

"Or very close cousin."

"Does Jake have any plans to rebuild his second barn? The one that burned?"

"Sometime in the future, he will. Oh, don't let me forget to go by the bank. I want to put your name on my accounts. And I think they have a policy that a husband's name has to be on his wife's account, too, even if it's separate. I promise you I'll never touch your money."

She smiled at him. "Silly man, I want you on my account. What if something were to happen to me? Yes, I definitely want you on it. We're married, you know."

Wes took a deep breath and grinned. "Nell, I need to tell you something. Remember the other day when you mentioned putting off the wedding ceremony? You said you thought we were on our way to being in love already. Well, I'm already there, sweetie. I love you."

Nellie leaned over and covered his cheek in kisses while she made wild, whooping noises. "Me, too, hon. I love you, too!"

Wes stopped the wagon for a quick kiss but it turned into a longer one. When he finally broke it, he took a deep, cleansing breath and said, "Whew! That was intense. It's going to take the rest of the trip into town for this baby to go back down."

"How likely is it we'll meet anyone else on this road?"

"Not likely at all. Probably zero chance of that happening."

Nellie got a wicked look on her face and told him to get the horses moving again. She unbuckled his belt, unbuttoned his buttons and freed his length. Then she lowered her head and gave Wes one of the most erotic experiences he'd ever had.

"HELLO, Shirley. Have you met my wife Nellie yet?"

"Yes, Bethie introduced us. Hello, dear."

Nellie returned the greeting.

"Shirley? Was that Mrs. Potter leaving? Was she crying?"

"Yes, it's bad news. I don't know if you know the Bonners, the couple who own the boarding house. Well, Mr. Bonner passed away in the night. Helen's not in good shape and depended on him to do a great deal for her. On top of losing a husband, she's worried about her future. It's so sad."

"I do know them. I stayed there a few days when I first came here. They were such a nice couple."

"Oh, yes, everyone in town thinks the world of them. They never had any children, you know. There's no one to take care of her now. No relatives."

"That's such a pity," Nellie said.

"I think Jim's calling for a men's meeting tonight. He'll probably try to find you. Might want to drop by the sheriff's office before you go home."

"Will do. Oh, by the way, I'd like to hire a woman to come

help do household chores two or three times a week. Do you know of anyone who might be interested?"

"I just might. Let me check around. If you'd like, you can put up a sign on the wall." Shirley reached under the counter and brought out a piece of paper, a pen, a bottle of ink, and a blotter.

"Thank you. Nell, why don't you pick up what we need, and I'll be writing a help wanted notice?"

When they left the general store, they headed to the restaurant. It was quieter than usual and Nellie wondered if it was because a townsman had died.

Arthur and Harriet Smithers were at the restaurant. As soon as she saw them, Harriet flagged them down. She took Nellie's hand when they got next to the table. "Will you two newlyweds be able to stop by our house on your way out of town? I promise I'll only keep you a few minutes. Less than a few minutes. I just want to give you a little gift. Just a token, but it's something important to Arthur and me."

Wes nodded. "Sure, we can. When we leave here, we still need to stop at the bank and the sheriff's office, but we can drop in as we leave."

Harriet squeezed Nellie's hand. "Perfect. Now you two go enjoy your lunch. We'll see you later."

When they sat down Nellie wondered aloud what that gift could possibly be. Harriet had described it as just a little token, yet it was something important to her and Arthur. They couldn't make sense of it and quit trying. They'd find out soon enough.

The trip to the bank was quicker than Wes expected. He'd been right; he had to be added to Nellie's account. They added Nellie to Wes' business account and his personal account. The old clerk who waited on them offered congratulations on their marriage. He said, "Well, you are now truly united in marriage. Access to the money, that's what cinches it."

They laughed politely at his joke that wasn't really funny and headed to Sheriff Larkin's office. When they arrived, they found a couple of other men discussing the passing of Mr. Bonner.

"Wes, I'm glad you dropped by. I was going to send a message to you and Jake. We're calling a men's meeting tonight. I know you haven't been involved in these meetings before, but you should be. The men are the ones who've been in town a long time or have proved successful in their business. They sort of act as a town council might. Advise on business matters and town planning. Do you think you can come? It's at the Community Hall."

"I'm sure I can."

"Good. Bring Jake. He's been to a couple of these before."

"All right, I will."

"Tell Jake about Bonner. One of the things we'll talk about is how the town can help Helen. Harriet has an idea she wants to throw out."

"Well, that should be interesting."

"It will. I've already talked to her a little bit. See you at seven."

"We'll be there."

They had one stop left, at the Smithers' home. Harriet answered immediately when Wes knocked.

"Come right in, folks, and have a seat. I promise, you'll be out in five minutes or less."

"All right, thank you," Nellie said and looked at Wes with a question in her eyes.

Arthur came in with a wooden box he handed to Nellie.

"This box is beautiful," she said.

Harriet looked happy that she thought so. "I think so, too. Angus Kelly makes these for us. Go ahead, open it."

Wes watched as his wife opened the box and took out the gift inside. When she had it unwrapped, she was stunned. *What have they given us?*

Wes didn't speak, either, so she had to. "You gave us... a... paddle?"

"Why, yes, dear, one engraved with your name on one side."

Nellie saw her name written backwards and realized it would leave the imprint of her name on her skin. She turned it over and saw the word *Obey* on the other side. It, too, was reversed.

"Well, thank you, um, but, um, why?" Nellie couldn't believe this was happening.

"We give one to each of the mail order bride couples to remind them to keep their priorities in order. That's paramount in a marriage; those vows need to be kept, especially the honor and obey one. Arthur and I discovered at the very outset of our relationship that he needs to keep me reined in. We've shared our experiences with all the other couples and a few other friends, and we're passing this on to you. Wes, it's up to you, of course, whether or not you intend to use this little jewel for its intended purpose. We strongly advise it. Arthur uses it on me, along with a whole host of other implements and devices. As a matter of fact, and pardon me for being a bit indelicate, but the use of these things has enhanced our physical relationship. If you choose not to use it for punishment, try using it for fun. You won't regret it."

Wes and Nellie were both dumbfounded. Neither knew what to say. Wes stammered something out. "This is interesting, very interesting indeed. Nellie and I will have to talk this over."

"Oh, yes, definitely do that. But, Nellie, ultimately you must respect Wes' decision. You must submit to him." Harriet smiled a mysterious smile. "It'll take you to new realms of ecstasy when you fully submit to him, truly submit. If you'd like to talk to me further, I'll be happy to share more. Arthur will, too." She stood then. "I won't keep you any longer. That would be very poor manners on my part since you're such new newlyweds. Think about what I said. It's a perfect time to try out this little gem."

They said the appropriate goodbyes and left. They were already turned off the main road before either of them spoke.

"I'm not sure what just happened," Nellie said.

Wes burst out laughing. "I'm not, either. Other than the fact that we just learned a couple of our most respected citizens have very odd lovemaking practices."

"Odd might not be a strong enough word," Nellie said.

"Maybe bizarre? Abnormal? Deviant? Unnatural?"

"Those all work. But really, paddling for fun? I don't understand."

"Maybe we should try it. You know, be adventurous, like Bethie said."

"I thought that meant something like doing it in the kitchen or maybe the barn. I didn't think she meant to bring in tools. I didn't know anybody did that!"

"Nellie girl, I've heard of toys in the bedroom. Never used any, though. I want to get some next time we're in a big town where they're available."

"Where would you buy those things? Surely, they don't sell them at a normal mercantile."

"No, they do not." He chuckled. "Some of your, um, better whorehouses have them to sell."

"I never dreamed of such."

"Are you still willing to be adventurous?"

"I said I would. If I don't like something, can we stop?"

"Most likely."

She eyed him suspiciously but shook her head and grinned.

Ruby ran out to meet them when she heard the horses. She stepped up to Nellie's side of the buggy and planned to help her step down when she saw the ornate box in the back seat.

"I see you've been visiting with Arthur and Harriet."

"Yes! They gave you one, too?"

"Indeed, they did. I thought it was a most unusual gift, didn't you?"

Both Wes and Nellie laughed. "You might say that."

Jake stepped out of the barn and called Wes to come see

something. "I'm headed to the barn with Jake, ladies, we'll see you later."

Nellie followed Ruby into the house.

"Let me put on a pot of coffee and I'll show you around the house. What did you think of what Harriet said?"

"It all sounded a bit preposterous to me. A paddle? And when she said she enjoys it for, you know, intimate purposes, I thought she must have lost a few marbles. I never heard of such."

"I hadn't, either. At first."

"Ruby? What do you mean?"

"You married my cousin. In my eyes, that makes us cousins. I look forward to us becoming close friends, too, Nellie. It'll be wonderful having a friend so close." Nellie agreed, and Ruby paused before she continued with her comments. "In anticipation of us being so close, we can share all our secrets. I'm going to share one with you. Harriet is absolutely right."

Nellie's eyes widened and she sharply drew in a breath. "You mean, you, I mean Jake, uses the paddle on you?"

"That and many other things. Let's let that sink in and I'll give you a tour of the house."

They did go through the house but Nellie's mind wasn't on decorations and furniture. When she saw a locked chest in their bedroom, she was curious but not enough to ask about it. Back in the kitchen, Ruby poured coffee and offered her cream and sugar.

"All right, we'll get back to the interesting things now," she said with a big grin. "You probably heard I was one big, problematic girl when I came here. I resented everyone and everybody and I especially resented being told I had to marry or go to prison. I suspected they were much the same. Nellie, I had no idea of the kinds of things that go on under our bright sun. Then I met Jake, and Harriet descended, and my world would never be the same."

"Well, you know I was a big behavioral problem, too," Nellie said.

"I know. That's why I'm telling you this. You might be like me and benefit in certain ways like I do. Respond to certain things like I do."

"I don't understand."

"It's hard to explain and make someone understand right off. Harriet asked me what I liked most about Jake, what I admired in him, what aspect of him I responded to. I had to think long and hard because I adore Jake. From the very first, I did. I thought of the times when I felt those flutters inside just because of something he said or did. That quickening of the heartbeat. The wetness down there."

Nellie couldn't believe Ruby was speaking so candidly, but she leaned forward to listen better. She didn't want to miss anything.

"I realized my strongest reactions were when he acted... his most masculine. When he took control both in and out of the bedroom, when he showed his confidence and his strength, his authority over me. It still makes me weak in the knees to think about him that way."

"Oh my," Nellie said. "I'm not sure I can relate to all that."

"Maybe you haven't been married to Wes long enough for those situations to come up. Pay attention. If he's stern or forceful or commands your attention when he speaks, think of how it makes you feel. If it sparks a response in you that turns you to squirming, submissive jelly, you might be more like Harriet and me than you imagine."

Nellie thought about the evening before when he'd told her in no uncertain terms that she wouldn't spend her money on livestock. He'd been stern then, unyielding. She didn't like that particular message, but she did like that strong aspect of him. Maybe there was something to this.

They heard footsteps clomping on the porch and Ruby

smiled and said, "For now, don't be afraid to play with the paddle. Keep it fun."

Nellie nodded hesitantly, indicating she would probably try it but with a little reluctance.

~

WHEN WES CAME home from the men's meeting that night, Nellie could tell he was upbeat.

"Tell me about the meeting, hon."

"Nell, that was the best meeting I've ever attended. It was called so the men could take some action to help out Helen Bonner since her husband passed. She had been especially worried since she's not as able to get around as she once was, and now there was no one to help her run the boarding house. Nobody to do chores, chop wood, that sort of thing. Apparently, she was worrying herself to a frazzle so bad, she couldn't even take a few minutes to mourn his death. The boarding house did a decent business and provided a modest living for them, but Miz Helen was petrified of what would happen to her when she was no longer able to cook for the people. Nellie, listen to me, sweetie. That just underscored what I told you last night. I want you to keep your money intact so you'll have it if something happens to me or to my ability to earn money. I never want to see Miz Helen's panic in your face. You hear me?"

"Yes, I can see how important it is, hon."

"Good. Anyway, Arthur and Harriet were there."

"Oh my word, no wonder it was an interesting meeting."

Wes laughed at that. "I thought that, too, but she came up with an idea that will not only help Miz Helen, but it'll address another problem we'll face soon. It's an excellent planning strategy. Matter of fact, the whole meeting was around planning town growth. It was exciting to hear all about it."

"Tell me! Tell me. This sounds interesting."

"All right. Harriet explained that they started out the mail order bride operation by having the ladies in town write to their own friends about marrying and settling here. But they've been so successful, articles are popping up about it here and there. Word's getting out. They're receiving mail from potential brides who don't know anyone here. Thus far, the women have stayed with their old friends until they marry. Where will the women stay who don't know anyone?"

"I can see that being a problem. Occasionally, a family might be able to take one in, but there might be more here at one time than we can handle."

"Exactly. So Harriet proposed that the town purchase the boarding house from Miz Helen and let her live there rent-free. That will give her some security for her future. She'll still cook and keep books as she does now, but the town will pay someone to do the caretaking and shopping and all the things Mr. Bonner did. They'll also pay Miz Helen a salary for her work."

"It's kind of heartwarming to see a town come together like that to help someone, to help their own."

"I thought so, too. I'm glad we ended up in this town. So, that's the part that helps Miz Helen, but the other part, the future planning part, calls for the men to build on to the boarding house and put in plenty of rooms for potential brides to stay until they marry. Harriet wants to call it the "Bride & Board." If the women end up not marrying and they get a job, then they can pay monthly rent. Otherwise, brides don't have to pay any boarding fees. Gann Douglas is already working on the expansion plans. I hadn't met him until tonight. He's Emmett's uncle and a building contractor man. I found out tonight that Gann and Emmett are unbelievably wealthy. They inherited from the original owner of the old silver mine."

"Emmett's that rich and he's a blacksmith?"

"Yes. They both only work because they enjoy it. By the way, he told me he's made the branding iron and he's finishing up the big metal sign. It'll be ready in two or three days. He said he'll bring it out here and help put it up. He'll bring everything we need."

"That's exciting! I can't wait to see it. Hollicker Hearts." She admired her wedding band again.

"It is exciting. But there's more. After Harriet and Arthur left to tell Helen the good news, the men continued talking about growth in the town, what businesses it could support and so on. Philip and Buck and Derek, all ranchers, you know, have been talking about taking cattle to the slaughterhouse in Laramie. They have to go a long way by train, and train travel isn't good for animals. They potentially lose a little money on each animal when it travels by train. So, they're thinking we could support our own slaughterhouse and processing plant. That would make way for a butcher shop or meat market in town, too. We're getting more and more people in who aren't hunters and there's a need. Especially since people are starting to use iceboxes out here. And that leads to another potential business we could use, an ice house. Right now, anybody who needs ice sends someone up one of these mountains in the summertime. In the wintertime, there's less demand, but there is some, so an ice house business will be seasonal to a certain degree, but they believe it would still support itself. It all makes sense. The have cooled train cars now that can carry the processed meat, and we can build insulated horse-drawn wagons to take the meat to the railroad. Think of it as putting meat on the train instead of the cows. It'll be a more efficient way to run the cattle business. It'll save money."

"Those are ambitious plans, Wes. When might they be carried out?"

"It's all still in planning stages, but Buck and Philip are determined to get a small slaughterhouse and meat processing place set up, maybe in time for next year's fall roundup. That means more jobs, too, so even more new men coming into town. More families."

"All that growth looks like it makes an opportunity for our business to grow, too. If we had more cattle when the slaughter-house is ready, we'd make more profit, wouldn't we?"

"Look at you, Nellie. I didn't realize you had such a head for business. But, yes, it's an opportunity for all the cattle ranchers."

"Maybe we should look at your growth plans for the ranch again. See if we can speed things up some."

"Look out, Nellie. We aren't dipping into our personal money."

Nellie sighed. "All right."

But her mind was running in circles thinking of things that might put them in a better position to take advantage of the growth.

LATER AS THEY were undressing for bed, Wes spotted the pretty wooden box in the closet where Nellie had placed it out of the way. He opened it and pulled out the paddle, admiring the work-manship a moment.

"Nell?"

"Yes?" she answered from across the room.

"Why don't we try this out?"

She saw what he held. "Are you asking for a reason why not? If you give me a minute, I can come up with one. Maybe more."

He chuckled at that. "No, really, come over here and let me swat you. I want to see what it's like."

Her mind swirled with the things Harriet and Ruby had said about playing with it.

"I'll let you swat me if you let me swat you. If you're going to wield it, you need to know how it feels."

"I grew up with a family who believed in not sparing the rod. I know what this kind of thing feels like."

"Not this particular one. And besides, I want to see my name written on your backside. Like it belongs to me."

"It definitely belongs to you, sweet cheeks. And I want to see *your* sweet cheeks with words on them, too. Look at this, sweetie. I'm already having a reaction here."

"I still don't understand how people can find this... conducive to that."

"Well, in all fairness, I was mostly thinking about your bare ass over my knee. Ever since we mentioned that before," he blew out a whistling breath, "that image in my head does things to me."

"Can I swat you first?"

"Sure. I'm too big to go over your lap. How about I bend over the bed?"

"All right." Already naked, he bent over and she came up behind and to the side of him. "This just feels so wrong. I'm not sure I can do it justice."

"What would you like to hit me for?"

"Well, nothing, Wes."

"Come on, Nell. If you can't, we can switch places right now."

"No, no. I want to see what it's like to use this thing."

"Make it count."

She hesitated.

"All right. Try this. Nellie, have I said anything that you disagreed with? Anything you didn't appreciate?"

"Well, yes, now that you mention it. I'm upset I can't invest my own money in our business, in the ranch. It's not fair. You say it's all my money, but you tell me how I can and can't spend it. I resent it."

"That's good; go with that. Because it's not changing. You spend your money on our livestock and I'll use that thing on you for real."

*Pop!*

"Youch," Wes said. "You can swing that thing pretty damn hard."

She waited.

"You can give me the second one now."

"I'm waiting for this one to show up better. I can barely see the outline of my name." Nellie rubbed all around on his skin where the paddle struck it. "All right, now I'm going to claim the other cheek. Ready?"

"Yes, ma'am. Do your worst."

Having had one under her belt and thinking of how much she resented not being able to use her own money, she swung back farther and popped a little wrist action at the last second.

"Ow!" Wes yelled. "Damn, woman, you must resent it a hell of a lot. That was hard. Although, I do like how you're rubbing it. That feels good." He stood.

"Wes! Look at that thing. It's hard again."

"What can I say?" He shrugged. "Now, hand me the paddle and take off your gown."

"Can't you just pull it up?"

"I could, but I don't want to. I'm naked. You should be, too."

She conceded and pulled the gown off. He sat on the bed and looked at her with a goofy grin, then patted his lap. Nellie giggled a little bit as she leaned over his lap.

"*Sweet Lord*, Nellie. Let's get Caleb to come out here and take a picture of this. What do you think about that? Forget our wedding day, this is the image I want to keep forever."

"If you want to keep drawing breath, I suggest you not do that."

"That's strong talk for someone who's over my lap. All nice and submissive. Compliant. I think I could get used to this."

*Submissive. That's the word Ruby used.*

"Are you ready? This is your first taste of it. I want it to be memorable."

"I don't think I'll have any problem remembering."

"Good girl." Wes caressed all over her bottom, then suddenly a loud cracking sound exploded in the room a split second before she felt it.

Nellie screamed out. It wasn't really a word, just a loud vowel sound.

"Wes! That was too hard! Oh, Lord, it hurts. Please don't do it again."

"Oh, but I have to. The other cheek needs to match. That was the *Nellie* side. Now I have to use the *Obey* side on your other cheek."

"Wait. Will you wait just a little bit? Let me recover from the first one?"

"I can do that," he said as he ran his fingers across the letters that were appearing. "I got you good. Your name shows up well. We'll have to tell Angus what a good job he did."

"I don't think so. Do you have to do the second one?" she said as she made a movement to lift herself up.

Wes saw the movement and put his hand on her back between her shoulder blades. He held firmly and she couldn't move. "You agreed, and besides, I'm running this show now. I've got you right where I want you, at my mercy. You'll get up when I say you can."

Nellie hadn't expected those words to come from her husband's mouth. She felt a twinge of her own and thought she might understand what Ruby meant when she said she liked it when Jake was at his most commanding and masculine. *But this is a game, remember? This isn't how Wes normally acts, not how he talks. He wouldn't be like this in a real situation. Right?*

"Nellie? I asked you something. Did you hear me?"

"I guess not."

"That'll cost you."

"Cost me what? I can't take a third lick with that thing!"

"You will if I say you will, little girl."

142

Nellie didn't know how to respond. That time, his voice matched his words and it was as though it was a real punishment. *He's getting into this.*

"Please?"

"All right. You can pay another way after you get the second lick."

"How?"

"I'll tell you when it's time. Get ready for your second strike now."

Nellie clenched her fists and her teeth, willing him to change his mind.

*Thwap!*

"Ow!" she yelled. After a moment she said, "I'm glad that's over," and began to lift up. Wes put his hand between her shoulder blades again.

"Not until I say so." He ran his fingers over the reddened spots, then enlarged his caressing area to include her upper thighs, delving into the split of her bottom. He put his hand between her legs and smiled at the wet state he found.

"I don't think you can make a critical comment on how hard I got when you got this wet."

"No, I didn't like it. At all. That's just because you were rubbing me."

"Tell yourself that all you want, baby doll. I know better." He continued to rub her skin, delving into the wet areas. "Now, Nellie, it's time for your extra penalty."

He pulled her up from his lap, stood, and pushed down on her shoulders. "Get on your knees and suck my cock."

*Yes, sir.* The words immediately came to her mind, but she didn't say them out loud. Wes pulled back her hair and held it out of the way so he could watch her. He occasionally pulled her hair or held it so she had to change her angle.

*Why the hell am I loving this so much?*

# CHAPTER 8

*J*t was fairly early in the morning when Emmett rode up, his wagon laden with the heavy metal sign. It was a big arch and they both knew it would look beautiful. He also brought all the supporting posts they needed and a shovel and post-hole digger.

"Emmett? Are you hungry? I can fix you some breakfast if you like."

"Oh, no, thank you. Lacy fixed me a big old breakfast before I left and I'm still about to pop. A little later on, though, I might like some coffee if it's no trouble."

"I'll go put it on as soon as I go back in. Right now, I want to make sure you men put this in the right place."

Both of the men laughed at that, but they got busy scoping out the driveway to find the best placement.

"One of the good things about having one of these is that it forces people to use a driveway. I can tell people pull their teams in the yard all along this stretch in front of the house," Emmett said. "You need to decide where you want your driveway to be. Before long you'll have an identifiable drive."

"Won't that make it look nice? Make it look like a real ranch business," Wes said.

"It's going to be beautiful. I love how it turned out. It's not just a sign, it's a work of art. I'm thrilled with it, Emmett."

"Thank you, ma'am, I'm glad you like it. Wes, grab that shovel. Once you decide where you want the drive, we need to measure for the holes. I make my signs extra wide so there's plenty of room for long teams and wagons to turn in. I've seen some too narrow to fit a big wagon."

All three of them agreed where they wanted the driveway and the sign. Nellie went back inside to make the coffee, then she sat on the porch and watched them work. She thought about how the sign would make the ranch look more like an established one, one that had been successful for a long time. Anyone who looked at that sign would be impressed.

*I wish that stubborn man would let me pitch in some money. I wouldn't have to spend much; I'd still have plenty left over to live on if the time comes. I wonder which account he used to pay for this sign. I'll be upset if I find out he used our personal one. It makes no sense that he won't let me buy a few more head of cattle. It's not like it would break us. I have all this money and can't touch it. It's not fair. Maybe by spring when it's time to get more cattle...*

*Wait. Maybe that's it, maybe I can do something else instead of buying more cattle. They'll take most of the current herd to market in the fall, then the winter will be slow until he gets more cattle in the spring. Unless he had dairy cattle. He said himself he wanted to use that piece of land across the road for dairy cattle. He said I can't buy cattle. What if find something else to help out that's not actually cattle? Loophole! Oh! Another loophole! He has a birthday coming up in a couple of weeks. I can say it's a birthday present that I knew he'd like. Has nothing to do with not sticking to that silly growth plan for the ranch. No. It's a birthday present. Nothing else.*

Nellie broke out in a big grin and went in the house, into the room he used as an office. She searched for some kind of land plat that would tell her how much land he had on that side of the road. She found it and wrote down the dimensions.

She took them each a cup of coffee and saw how much progress they'd made. She had to admit, it was going to be striking. It was the perfect touch, a nice focal point from the road. She could imagine detailing driving paths to the house and to the barn, instead of how it was now, with no differentiation between path and yard. It was already an attractive place, but this would be so much better. It wouldn't be quite the showplace Philip and Bethie's ranch was, but it would be nice.

After Emmett left later that morning, Nellie and Wes stood back to admire the new banner sign. They were both thrilled with it. She told him her idea of perhaps having established driving paths and parking areas for the barn and the house, how she thought it would make it look more attractive, more like the cleaner look of Philip's place. Wes agreed, especially since he was the main one driving and parking.

"Wes, I'd like to ride out to Bethie's and visit a while. Is that all right with you?"

"Sweetie, I can't afford the time. Putting that sign up got me behind on some chores that need to be done. I can't go."

"I could still go. I can ride a horse. Quite well, in fact. I've been riding all my life. I know the way, so it's not like I could get lost. And I'll be home in time to make supper. Is it all right if I go?"

He thought about it a few moments. "Can you shoot a gun?"

She grinned. "Daddy and I used to have shooting contests. Bring me a gun and I'll show you."

"I don't really want you to go, but dang it, I can't think of a good reason why you can't. Promise me you'll be extra careful, all right? Don't want my girl to have any problems."

She brightened with excitement. "I won't! Thank you." Nellie planted a big kiss on his lips and turned to head to the house, then she turned back. "One thing, I can ride a horse until the cows come home, but I've never saddled one myself. Would you do that for me?"

Wes laughed. "Yes, ma'am, I will. But I'll be teaching you how real soon."

Nellie freshened up and grabbed her reticule and one of Wes' six-shooters from the gun cabinet. She checked that it had bullets and put it in her bag. Wes helped her up on the saddle and kissed her again, and she was off.

Nellie was almost giddy with her plan. Wes might not let her get away with this little plot scot-free, but she had solid reasons on her side to at least try to argue her position. *So what if I get in trouble? Pain doesn't last forever. And we'll be that much ahead on the ranch expansion. Once it's done, he can't exactly get rid of it.*

There was no one outside at Ruby's house, so she rode on by. It was a fairly quick trip into town and she was still smiling. She slowed down in town, wanting to check the popular places for Philip and Bethie's wagon. After all, Bethie had no idea she was coming and it was possible they weren't even home. She had to go there, though, if only for a few minutes, to keep from lying to Wes. She said she was going to visit Bethie, and that was the first thing she needed to do. As she neared the mercantile, sure enough, she saw their wagon. She tethered her horse to one of the rails in front and went inside.

Bethie was inside paying for her purchases. "Nellie! It's so good to see you. Is Wes with you?"

"No, he couldn't get away. I told him I wanted to come visit with you. Since you didn't know I was coming, I thought I'd better check in town before riding all the way out there."

"Good thing you did, girlie. Philip's tied up at the telegraph office. I told him I'd be at the restaurant when I got all the groceries. Let's go on over there and get something to drink."

"All right, sounds good."

"Let me get these things in the wagon."

"You'll do no such thing," Shirley said. "Clint can do that. You and Nellie get on over there now."

They both thanked Shirley and headed across the road.

"Do you want to order food now or wait until Philip gets here?" Nellie asked.

"Let's wait. Surely, he won't be long. Tell me how married life's going. Is it as good as I told you?"

Nellie's grin told the story. "Yes, I was silly to be worried. It's been wonderful. I can tell Wes is happy, too. Sometimes I still can't believe how much my life has changed, and so fast. I don't think I'd recognize the old me. I feel like a whole different person."

"That's such wonderful news. I know your father would be so proud and so happy for you."

Nellie nodded. "I think so, too."

"So why are you out today? Was there something special you wanted to talk to me about?"

Nellie laughed. "I don't actually need to talk to you about anything. I needed an excuse to come to town on my own, so I told Wes I wanted to visit you. But I didn't want to lie, so I had to find you so we could visit. Then I'll do what I really came to town to do."

"Which is?"

"Buy Wes a birthday present. It's a surprise, so you can't mention it."

"Well, that's fun. Everybody loves surprises."

Nellie's facial expression clearly said "maybe not" and Bethie told her to fess up.

She lowered her voice so no one else could hear and explained the situation and her rationalization for possibly getting away with it.

"You realize you're going to get your backside torn up, don't you?"

"Maybe not."

"That sentence I just said? Play like I just said it again. Torn. Up."

"All right, maybe," Nellie said.

"Let me say it again. T. O. R. N up."

Nellie sighed. "All right. Probably. But by then it'll be done and I'll have what I want, helped Wes get ahead of his plan, and given him a birthday present that will actually be useful. I'll do my best to get by with it, but if I don't, then so be it."

Bethie eyed her again. "Do you hear yourself? 'You'll have what you want?' It might be that you aren't as far away from the old you as you think you are."

Nellie felt the sting of that. Was that what she was doing? Rebelling so she could get her way? No. No, she was making improvements to their business. She was actually saving time by doing something that might have been a delay later. There.

"No, I don't think so. Maybe he won't see it that way. But I'll probably have to be careful about what I say and how I defend myself. I don't want to slip up like that again."

Philip joined them and seemed genuinely happy to see Nellie. He, too, asked her how married life was going.

She told him how happy they were and how well everything was working out. She mentioned the new banner sign that Emmett had made and how good it looked. Bethie was excited about it and promised they'd come soon to see it.

"So what brings you into town while your poor groom is at home working his fingers to the bone?" Philip asked.

She glanced at Bethie. "His birthday is in a couple of weeks, and I wanted to surprise him with a gift for the ranch. Promise me you won't tell him. I don't want to spoil the surprise."

"I promise, I won't. What are you getting?"

She explained that she wanted to buy the fencing materials for the land across the road from the house that would be for the dairy side.

"He wasn't planning to do that until late next year, possibly even the next. Why do you want to jump the gun?"

"To accelerate his plans to expand. You know about how much land he has. Do you have any idea how much that'll cost? Here. Here are the dimensions."

Philip took out a little pad of paper and a pencil and did some figures. "This is what it'll be for materials only. Will Wes be digging all these holes himself, or do you want the mill to provide labor?"

"Oh, I hadn't thought of that. I don't want to buy him more work to do, especially after altering his overall plan. Yes, include labor."

"Let's figure two men doing the work and several days to get it done. This is what you're looking at. It's just a general estimate; it could be more or it could be less."

"Ooh. That's a little more than I planned, but it'll be worth it to get the work done for him. Let me ask you this. How much would it cost to build the dairy barn?"

Philip took the paper and added some more figures. "For the type of barn Wes wants, it'll run about this much. That's not counting any milking supplies or equipment."

"Oh, I think a barn may have to wait. Although, what use is a fence if you don't have a barn?"

"Does Wes have any idea you're doing this?"

"None at all, and please don't tell him," Nellie said.

"Nellie, you realize this isn't the same as surprising him with a pair of new boots. Wes is an organizer, a planner, and he's good at it. Are you sure he's going to appreciate you coming in here and stepping all over his schedule?"

"Possibly not, but if I go ahead and do it, we'll still be that much ahead next year. We'll be able to move faster."

"Let me go on record and say it's a bad idea, Nellie. I hate to disappoint you, but I think you should go for the new boots under the circumstances. I'm not sure how Wes is going to respond to this particular surprise."

"I'll think about it. Meanwhile, I'll go over to the sawmill and get exact figures on the fence." She saw the look on Philip's face and added, "Just to check it out."

"All right. Talk to Angus Kelly. He might cut you a deal."

"I know that name."

Philip laughed. "He makes the paddles for all the mail order couples. Harriet pays him to make them."

"Oh, no," Nellie said, shoulders drooping. "You know about those?"

"Know about them? He had one specially made for me!" Bethie interjected.

"Yes," Philip answered. "His wife Nessa is Bethie's friend from childhood. She told Bethie about them. I take it you have yours already?"

"Yes. And that's all I'll say about it."

Philip laughed as they said their goodbyes and Nellie headed for the sawmill.

ON THE RIDE HOME, Nellie pulled out the sales slip and tried to quell the earthquake going on in her belly. *Too late now, Nellie. You have to live with it. Well, there's an outside chance he'll be happy about it. At least in time. Probably not in time to save the skin of my ass, though. Oh, Nellie, why did you do this? Did you really just want to get your own way again?*

The thought troubled her more than she wanted to admit.

*You've got a few days before it'll be delivered. Figure this thing out, girl. What'll you tell him?*

WES AND NELLIE sat side by side on the couch that evening after the supper dishes were cleaned and the kitchen tidied up.

"Sweetie, remember when we talked about being able to say things to each other even though they were embarrassing?" he asked.

"I remember."

"I think I'm about to be embarrassed. There's something I want to talk about."

"You can say anything to me, hon, what is it?"

"Please try to keep an open mind. You have a stake in this, too." Wes squeezed her hand.

"All right. This sounds serious."

"It's important to me, to us and our intimate life. Just two things, really. The other night when we played with that paddle, I liked it. I mean, I really liked it. Having you over my lap, with you helpless, having to take what I dished out, that was incredibly exciting to me. And seeing your body like that, I wasn't kidding when I said that was the image I wanted to keep forever. The feeling I got from exercising that kind of control while you submitted yourself to me, was something I have never felt before. I don't want that to be a one-time thing. I want to do that again."

"Every time?"

"No, just occasionally. I want us to keep that scenario in our repertoire, so to speak. Would you be willing to do that?"

"Do you have to wield that thing quite as hard as you did?"

"Not if we're playing."

Her face drained when she remembered the sales slip from the sawmill. *That won't be playing.*

"That means you would do it for real?"

"I told you before we were married if I think it's necessary, I'll do it. But, sweetie, you've been my angel. I don't see that on the horizon anywhere. Don't worry about it. Besides, admit it, you got pleasure from it, too. You were soaking wet."

"I told you, that was because you were rubbing me."

"We both know better. Do you think we could include that now and then?"

"Yes, all right."

"When are you going to admit you enjoyed it some?"

"I didn't enjoy the pain at all," Nellie said.

"Then what made you so wet?"

"My turn to be embarrassed. Don't laugh at me."

"I wouldn't do that anyway, and I especially wouldn't do it when we're talking about our sex life. Come on. You can tell me anything. What did you like about it?"

"I liked the control you had. The strength you showed. Like you knew what you wanted and you were going to make sure you got it—making me submit, making me want to submit."

"Whew, Nellie. It sounds like we were made for each other."

Nellie grinned and nodded. "But I don't want it to be like that every time. Just sometimes."

"I agree. Besides, it might get old otherwise." He shrugged. "I might get bored having a woman cater to my every whim all the time."

"Smart aleck."

"Well, I've got one more thing to talk about."

Nellie laughed. "Gotta be better than that last one."

Wes smirked. "You might think so, but probably not. I told you about what it was like in college. There were prostitutes, there were loose women, and even willing women who weren't really loose. There was something we did back then. I mean, young people in general, that was fairly common because the woman couldn't get a baby from it."

"Really? What's that?"

"It's a way to keep the man from spilling his seed inside her. Instead of using a woman's normal channel, we had anal sex instead."

"What? No. You mean you want to put that thing in my... my backside?"

"That *thing* is my cock, and, yes, I want to do exactly that. It is highly erotic for both partners, and it feels... it feels so tight in a different way. I'll make sure you find your release, too, just like we do now. As many times as you want."

"Isn't it, oh, Wes, I don't even know how I can say it."

"Try. You can say anything to me."

"Isn't it... dirty, doing it that way."

"It is. But that's what soap and water are for. I'll be the one getting dirty; you don't even have to see it."

"That would be so humiliating. I know it would."

"You don't know it, that's just what you think right now. If I told you I could give you a kind of pleasure you never felt before, wouldn't you be interested?"

"Probably. Will you at least ease me into it?"

He smirked and it had a hint of evil in it. "I'll have you begging me for it."

"I would bet not. But as long as you don't hurt me, well, I can try. How soon do you want to do that?"

"We'll work up to it. I'll start with just touching you there, working up a little more each time. What you'll find is that it's an incredibly sensitive spot. It can give you amazing pleasure."

"Promise me you'll have soap and water and cloths at the ready."

Wes laughed. "I promise. Now come here and kiss me. I thank you so much for talking about these things. And I thank you even more for being willing to do the things I like. Tell me what you'd like and I'll move mountains to satisfy you," he ended up, whispering his words.

What followed was the sweetest, purest, and most tender lovemaking they'd had yet, and they felt closer than they'd ever been.

~

THE DAY NELLIE dreaded finally came. Wes had ridden into town for something for an injured horse, so he wasn't there when the wagonloads of fencing lumber arrived. She was even more anxious when she saw just how much wood there was.

She showed the men the lot and pointed out the stobs that indicated the property line. One of the men explained that they put fences a few feet inside the line. It was the custom. Since she didn't know where the barn would go, she couldn't tell them where she wanted the gate to go. "Do you really have to know that now?"

"No, ma'am. We build the gates on the location because they'd be too big to haul in a wagon. We brought all the lumber and hardware. We can build it when we're ready for it or when we know where it'll go. The first thing we usually do is plant the fence poles around the perimeter. Then we go back and put the cross pieces that make it a fence. We'll set the front fence back a bit to allow wagons and such in front of it. That's what most ranchers want. Well, all of them I know."

"All right, then," she said. "I guess you can go ahead and get started on it."

"Ma'am, are you sure you don't want us to wait on your husband and let him tell us where he wants everything?"

"No, it's supposed to be a surprise for his birthday. Besides, he's gone into town and I'm not sure how long he'll be. Not long, I expect. Do you have any idea how long it'll take to get the job completed?"

"Depends on the ground mainly. If all goes well, we'll be out of your way inside of a week."

"I see. Well, thank you. I'll be in the house if you need me."

*Great. Now he'll not only be angry with me, he'll be reminded every day for a week how angry he is. Or 'inside of a week,' whatever that means. You'll be lucky if he doesn't break that paddle on you.*

155

She sat at the kitchen window and watched the men. It looked like they decided to wait a little longer to see if Wes arrived and could give them better instructions. They started putting the gate together.

*Why did I ever think I could get away with this? Admit it. Admit it to yourself. It's because he told you not to spend your money on livestock. This is just another wild idea of yours, another time when you had to get your way. You had to prove something and the devil hang whoever got in your way. You haven't changed, Nellie. Face it. This is the real you. Spoiled and manipulative. Determined to get your way and show everyone else that you can. This is going to hurt Wes to the core. He trusted you.*

The sobs started when she finally admitted it to herself.

She heard Wes' horse before they completed the gate. She splashed her face with water and dried it, dabbing at her eyes to remove the tears. She went back to the window and waited for him.

He dismounted and introduced himself to the workers, shaking their hands. She couldn't make out the words, but so far, he didn't sound angry. His voice wasn't raised. She saw the first worker—she didn't even remember his name—pull a folded piece of paper out of his pocket. Even from the window, she recognized it as the carbon copy of the sales receipt she had, with her signature prominently displayed.

Wes turned to face the house and called out her name. She didn't want to make him wait. She ran outside and hurried to them.

"I understand this is a surprise for my birthday. Is that right?"

"Yes, I wanted to get you something I knew you wanted, something you planned to get anyway, in time, something for the ranch." Nellie swallowed nervously. "Don't you like it?"

"It looks like it'll be a fine fence. Give me a few minutes to talk to these men about the gate and fence lines, and I'll be in to talk about this. Be ready to discuss it with me."

"I will."

*Damn.*

This wasn't going to be a kitchen table discussion, open and airy. No, this one would be a bedroom discussion, and not the good kind. It would be serious, intense, and intensely private. Wes would be angry that she disobeyed and spent her money, disappointed in her willfulness, betrayed and heartbroken that she didn't simply share with him what she wanted to do and why. He would be so disillusioned that her old behavior had appeared again.

She was disillusioned with herself. His disappointment couldn't be worse than hers, she realized. She shook her head and it made new tears roll down her face.

*I deserve everything he could do to me.*

Nellie retrieved the paddle from the box in the closet and sat on the bed with it. She heard the front door open and close, then she heard his footsteps. She braced herself.

"We need to have a serious conversation, Nellie."

"Yes. I know."

"Tell me what made you think it was acceptable to do this after I specifically said not to spend your money."

"Well, specifically," she repeated his word, "you said I couldn't spend it on livestock. You didn't say I couldn't spend it on a fence."

He chuckled but it was a hollow one. "I don't know whether to think that's clever or duplicitous."

"At the time, I thought it was clever."

"I imagine you did." Wes walked over, pulled up a chair directly in front of her, then sat down. He leaned forward but not in a threatening way. It looked like he was interested in what she had to say for herself. "I explained my reasoning for why I didn't want you to use your own money for the ranch. I was clear. Did you really think that just because I didn't specifically mention fencing, it was a permissible exclusion to my wishes?"

"Not when you put it like that. I was hoping I could get you to see it my way."

"Then why didn't you just talk to me and try to make me see it your way?"

"I tried to talk to you about it. You just said no, not to buy livestock."

"All right, I'll have to own up to that. Maybe I didn't give you enough of a chance to discuss it and possibly get me to see your reasoning. In the future, I'll be sure to give you a chance to persuade me instead of just cutting you off. I'll try to be more open."

"Thank you."

"But this time, I said no, and I said it to the point where there shouldn't have been any doubt. That's the situation we're dealing with right now. I laid down a directive and I expected you to adhere to it. Instead, you defied me. That shows disrespect, even contempt, not only for me, but for the very relationship we're trying to build together. What is this doing to our trust?"

Her face twitched and quivered as she tried not to dissolve into tears. "You probably don't know if you can trust me or not."

"Can I?"

"This is me, Wes. It's how I've always been. I wanted to do something, spend my money on something for the ranch that you told me not to do. And, yes, you were clear. I just wanted to prove I could get my own way. I mean, I didn't think that consciously or in those words, but that's how it works out. It's what it looks like when it's all said and done. I never have been one to say or even think something like 'I'll show you' or 'I'm going to do it anyway,' but if you look at my choices, I might as well have been thinking that way. It might be better if I did. I just make myself look like a conniving witch."

"Oh, and you lied to me about where you were going that day. You said you were going to visit with Bethie."

"But I did visit with Bethie. It wasn't a lie."

"Yes, but it was just a pretext. The reason you went to town wasn't to visit, was it? It was to go to the sawmill. It's a lie as far as I'm concerned."

"But I couldn't because I wanted it to be a surprise."

"And we're back to the duplicity again. It was never about a birthday surprise, was it?"

"No."

"What are your thoughts right now?"

"How can I answer that? I'm ashamed and embarrassed, humiliated. I'm sorry that my old habits are coming out again. I thought I was leaving them behind. Mostly, I'm sorry for the damage to us. I want your trust again."

"I'm glad to hear that. I want it, too. I'd like to see us come out of this even stronger than we were."

"I want that, too. More than you can know."

"I believe you, sweetie, but we still need to deal with this. You know there have to be consequences."

Nellie nodded her assent. She slowly handed him the paddle.

"This one will be real, you know that. Right?"

"I know. I already decided I deserve whatever you think is appropriate."

"Good girl. I'm proud of you for not fighting me on this. I think you might as well take your clothes off."

"All of them?"

"Yes."

"But—"

"All of them, Nell. Are you going to defy me again?"

"No, I won't."

"That's my good girl."

He watched her remove her clothing. She'd undressed in front of him many times, but she'd never felt this exposed before, this vulnerable.

"Over my knee now. Sweet Lord, Nellie. I almost hate to turn this thing red. Almost. Get situated as comfortably as you can. It'll be bad enough as it is. And don't put your hands back to protect yourself; they could get hurt pretty bad. Are you ready?"

"As ready as I'll ever be."

"All right."

The first blow surprised her. She hadn't recovered from that one when the next one hit. She yelled with the third one, then the fourth. She pounded her fist on the lower part of the chair Wes sat on. He continued the strokes and she continued to blubber, unable to make words.

Finally, he stopped and she lay there, limp.

"Almost done, sweetie. These last two are going to hurt the most, then it'll be over."

They were delivered so fast and so furiously hard that she couldn't even get a scream out until moments after the second one landed. They were placed in that tender crease where bottom meets legs. She'd likely be reminded of them for days.

Wes stroked her back with his left hand, gently shushing her. He set the paddle down on the bed and, with a delicate touch, tried to comfort her bottom. She hissed at first but he continued until she felt the worst of the pain begin to subside. "Come on, sweetie, come up here in my arms."

She welcomed the feel of them after her punishment and remembered that from the very first time she met him, his arms made her feel safe and secure.

Wes grabbed a quilt from the foot of the bed and wrapped it around her. He stroked her hair and gently rocked her back and forth just enough to be soothing. Soon, she calmed.

"Sweetie, I'm proud of you. Thank you for yielding yourself to me."

"I owed you that much."

"Speaking of things owed, I thought of a way for you to replace the money you spent from your account."

That got her attention. "I have to replace it? It's really only a fraction of the total amount in the account. There's still plenty of money left."

"Maybe so, but this is how it's going to be."

"How can I replace it? I don't make any money."

"I've given it some thought. Right now, I'm willing to pay a woman to come in two or three times a week to help with household chores. Instead, you'll do everything she would have done, and the amount of money I would have paid her will go toward your debt."

"But—"

"Consider it a continuation of your punishment. No argument. No negotiation. Most women don't have household help anyway. And no slacking. I'll check."

Nellie did some mental calculation. "Wes, at that rate, it'll take a year or more to pay back the money. Is there any way we can speed that up? Anything else I can do?"

He smirked again. "I thought about that, too. There is something else. This one you have control over. You can say no if I instigate it, and you can ask for it if you want to make money toward your debt. It's up to you."

"I want to pay the money back as soon as possible. I don't want this hanging over me. Tell me what I can do."

"The other night I told you about some things that give me pleasure. One was having you over my knee, willing to submit to me, surrendering to my control. It might not always be a paddling over my knee, but it'll be my desires and your obedience. It might be harsh; it might not. The other thing was anal penetration, which you already agreed to try anyway. Now you can lower the debt each time."

"Will that be harsh, too, or will you still try to be gentle and make it pleasurable for me?"

"I never want that one to be painful or harsh. Pleasure only."

"How much would you pay me for those things? Will I think it's worth it to pay back my account?"

"I'll pay you the same thing a prostitute would charge. And I always tipped well."

When she found out the amount for each, she agreed.

"So I can say no if I don't want to do it, or if I want to earn more, I can let you know and we'll do... whichever I choose at the time. What if you don't want to? Will I get the money anyway by default?"

"Not going to happen, sweetie. I will want to. Guaranteed."

# EPILOGUE

The fence turned out beautifully. With the new Hollicker Hearts sign flying across the entrance, the whole ranch looked impressive. It inspired success and a successful attitude in them both.

Nellie convinced Wes to go ahead and splurge and build the dairy barn, and he was glad he did. It cut his overall schedule from a three year plan to a two year plan. They worked together, working long, hard hours, and readied the new barn and pasture for the dairy cattle. Philip delivered a small herd of milk cows shortly after his other cows were taken to slaughter and just before winter weather set it. Nellie discovered she loved the dairy business and spent a good deal of time with the cows whenever she had free time. That is, when she wasn't doing the extra housework or asking Wes to allow her to lower her debt in a more carnal way. He'd been right, though. She did beg him for it. They both liked the arrangement so well, they continued it even after she'd replaced the money in her account.

He made good on his promise to take her on a honeymoon. They chose San Francisco. On their first day there, Nellie waited at the hotel while Wes found a couple of particularly interesting

whorehouses that sold novelty items to increase marital pleasure, if the advertisements were to be believed. There were
marital aids and medical aids and punishment implements and
clamps and plugs and things even Wes wasn't sure of. He bought
them all and even had to purchase an additional bag to pack
them in for the trip home. They didn't see a single play or show
on their honeymoon, nor did they do any shopping. They rarely
left their room, only occasionally going out to eat. Mostly, they
had food sent up. But they were determined to be well
acquainted with their new toys, or tools, before they went home.

Harriet would be proud.


## The End


*NORA'S NOTE:* Do you think it's unlikely that Bethie could have
brought home the wrong cow? That tidbit had a real-life inspi-
ration. Let me tell you a similar anecdote that's part of my family's treasury of memories. It was during the Great Depression
and my mother's family was fortunate enough to own a cow.
Their yard wasn't always the best place for it, though, so sometimes they let it graze in a friend's pasture down the road. Late
one afternoon, my grandfather sent two of my aunts to retrieve
the cow. They were a tween and a young teen at the time, and if
you can believe their telling of it, they had done this task before
and done it successfully. They were a little late getting back and
Granddad began to worry, but he soon heard them return. He
went out to take the cow from them to see to it for the night and
couldn't believe the sight in front of him. It wasn't their cow. It
didn't even resemble their cow. Oh, Granddad wasn't happy. Not
at all.

We've heard this tale so many times through the years and it always makes us laugh until we almost cry. Just the thought of those two girls struggling with a cow that wasn't familiar with them, having a hard time getting it roped so they could lead it, and poking and prodding and coaxing and sweet-talking the poor thing to make it leave with them. I'd give anything if we'd recorded my aunts telling it in their own words.

# NORA NOLAN

Nora Nolan is one of my pen names. It's nice to meet you! I love to read all kinds of books. All kinds! So far, though, I've only written one basic type. They usually have fairly normal, sexy, fun relationships between the main characters, infused with a little wicked kink. So if you like age play, strong D/s lifestyles, or women in chains who beg to be caned, you might want to look for other authors. I'm not there yet.

My newest joy is sitting at the keyboard letting the characters in my head write their stories. They often lead me in directions that surprise me. I never know when I start out what direction they'll take or where they'll end up.

I live in the southern central part of the US. My happier days find me with our family, or spending time with my wonderful alpha husband.

Email Nora directly at NoraNolan.books@gmail.com
Website: https://www.noranolanbooks.com

Don't miss these exciting titles by Nora Nolan and Blushing Books!

*Operation Big Rock Brides (Historical Western)*
Two Brides for Big Rock
Opal from Omaha
Ruby from Rawlins
Lacy from Laramie
Nellie from Newport

# BLUSHING BOOKS

Blushing Books is the oldest eBook publisher on the web. We've been running websites that publish steamy romance and erotica since 1999, and we have been selling eBooks since 2003. We have free and promotional offerings that change weekly, so please do visit us at http://www.blushingbooks.com/free.

# BLUSHING BOOKS NEWSLETTER

Please join the Blushing Books newsletter
to receive updates & special promotional offers.
You can also join by using your mobile phone:
Just text BLUSHING to 22828.

Every month, one new sign up via text messaging will receive a
$25.00 Amazon gift card, so sign up today!